King of Hearts

MARK STIBBE

malcolm down

PUBLISHING

22 21 20 19   7 6 5 4 3 2 1

First published 2019 by Malcolm Down Publishing Ltd.
www.malcolmdown.co.uk

British Library Cataloguing in Publication Data
A catalogue record for this book is available from the British Library.

ISBN 978-1-910786-39-0

Cover design by Esther Kotecha
Art direction by Sarah Grace

Printed in Great Britain by Bell and Bain Ltd, Glasgow

Life is not a matter of holding good cards but playing a poor hand well.

Robert Louis Stevenson

Contents

Acknowledgements

I want to thank those who have heard versions of this story over the years and who have offered words of warm and effusive encouragement. I am especially grateful to the late Helen Clark, who was overwhelmed the first time I read out a short story version of this novel to her and others in 2011. Helen always believed in the power and impact of this story and it is to her that I dedicate this novella. I wish she had been alive to see its publication but I know that one day we will be able to celebrate together, in the grand and vast library of the Father's House. Thank you Helen, and Philip (Helen's late husband), for never ceasing to believe in me, even when – like Jake – I lost the plot for a while.

In addition, I'd like to thank George, Juliette, Matt, Cat and Tim for their invaluable help in the research I did for a first version of this story, *The Prodigal Father*. I'd also like to thank Malcolm Down, Sarah Griggs and Esther Koetcha for their invaluable help in preparing and publishing this present volume, and my son Sam for the internal drawings at the start of each chapter. Last but by no means least, I am eternally grateful to my beloved wife Cherith who has helped at every stage, especially with the proofreading.

1. A Blast from the Past

It was just after breakfast on Christmas Eve and Jake Graystone was about to make the worst decision of his life.

Three months earlier, he had been driving home from work on a blustery autumn day. One hour before, he had been summoned to the principal's office at the college where he had spent two decades marking textbooks and time. The principal, a woman with a penchant for power dressing, had asked him to sit down while she smoothed the creases out of her black suit jacket. She had mumbled about the threat of a double-dip recession before lamenting about the stress she was now carrying because of the demands put upon her by local government. Jake heard mention of 'cost-cutting' and 'new targets' but all the while his eyes were drawn to the window of the office, where heavy raindrops were flecking the glass, now stained with clinging, autumn leaves.

As the principal continued, Jake felt a tightening in his chest. The woman in the suit was at last arriving at the point, moving with a practiced art from the political to the personal, explaining with a careful gravity that all the departments in the college were now under review, including Jake's, and that no job within these departments was safe from scrutiny or termination... including Jake's.

The woman's voice now became dull and distant, like the sound of a far-off drill biting into a pavement. Jake's focus was not on cuts and reviews. It was on his bank account, depleted by the cost of providing private tuition for his younger son, who two years before had been diagnosed with dyspraxia. Jake had not had a pay rise in five years and he and his family were already living hand-to-mouth.

The principal looked at her watch and rose to her feet behind the cluttered desk, signalling the end of the short meeting.

'HR will review your job after Christmas,' she said.

Jake drove into the village that had been his home since he had met and married Sally fifteen years before. His mind was now a blizzard; one moment a gust of fearful forebodings, the next a squall of desperate calculations. His family had already reduced their outgoings. If new income did not soon stream into their lives, their accounts would run dry and their prospects would be bleak once Christmas had come and gone.

As Jake clenched the steering wheel, he noticed the sign of his local pub swaying in the wind. He had a five-pound note in his pocket, given to him by a lanky student who had paid him back for money borrowed on a college outing to the science museum. For a moment, he thought of heading home and giving it to Sally, but then, before he knew it, he was in the car park of The Tempest, walking to the bar, ordering a pint of ale, and looking for somewhere to sit and collect his thoughts.

It was then he saw him.

Jake hadn't seen Pete Marley for over twenty years, not since university days, but there he was sitting in a corner, drinking whiskey from a tumbler and reading a broadsheet newspaper.

'Is that you Pete?'

The man looked up. After the faintest hint of confusion, his face shifted from recognition to a broad grin. 'Jake Graystone!' Pete was standing now. 'You've not changed a bit!'

'Apart from a few grey hairs,' Jake replied as he shook Pete's hand.

'Are you here to meet someone?' Pete asked.

'No.'

'Then pull up a chair.'

Jake drew up a short stool to Pete's table. 'What brings you here?' Jake asked.

Pete folded up his newspaper. 'Poker.'

'In The Tempest?'

'First time for me here, but I've played in the backrooms of many pubs. Most evenings… in casinos and private homes, too.'

'You must have an understanding wife!' Jake joked.

'Divorced,' Pete replied. 'Twice.'

Just then, Jake noticed a change in Pete's expression, as if a synapse of memory had fired somewhere in the hidden pathways beneath his greased-back, jet-black hair.

'You married Sally Jenkins, didn't you?'

'I did,' Jake replied.

'I dated her at school. When you were boarding.'

Jake coughed. 'I didn't know that…'

'How was boarding school, by the way?'

'Better than home,' Jake replied.

'Really? I always kinda felt sorry for you.'

'It was just Mum, by then she was bipolar. She said I was too much of a handful, so she packed me off to a minor public school. Harsh, but definitely better than home.'

'Didn't it affect you?'

Jake thought for a moment.

'Sally says I don't show my emotions,' he said. 'I guess I learned not to. Part of my survival kit.'

Pete nodded. 'You and Sally still together?' he asked.

'Yes.'

'And how is your mum?'

'Suicide. Last year.'

'I'm sorry.'

The two men endured an awkward silence.

It was Jake who spoke first. 'What are you doing these days?'

'Poker, full time,' Pete replied. 'The cards have put the shine back into my life.'

At the mention of the word 'shine', Jake noticed the glitter of a band on Pete's right hand. It was shaped like a signet ring and on it was engraved the outline of a shark. Underneath was inscribed the word, Mako.

'What's with the bling?'

Pete laughed. 'Poker players adopt a nickname. Part of the image...'

'But why a shark? I don't recall you being into marine biology.'

'I caught one once. Early seventies. Off Padstow. In the days when sharks hadn't been overfished and when you could catch Porbeagle sharks and even a Mako.'

'Off the British coast?'

'Yep. One time I chartered a boat, went out twelve miles into the Gulf Stream, put out some chum, set two 50 lb fishing lines and waited.'

Pete paused for effect as he lifted the glass of shimmering whiskey to his lips.

'About midday one of the lines started to run. I can still remember the screaming of the reel like it was yesterday. The hairs on the back of my neck were bristling.'

Pete put his glass down.

'The skipper took charge. He buckled a butt strap around my waist and inserted the rod into it. He told me to keep the pressure on. The shark responded by running even further from the boat.'

Pete looked down at his ring, took it off and held it for a moment.

'The skipper and his mate were becoming very animated and were barking instructions at me not to let up for a moment. I was fit, but I wasn't anything like as strong as that fish and the muscles on my arms were already aching.'

'How on earth did you keep going?'

'Everything changed when we saw what it was. One moment it was underwater and the next moment it breached. All of us gasped. It was at least eight feet long. It was a Mako!'

Jake was wide-eyed now.

'For two-and-a-half hours I pulled while the Mako ran and breached. And then at last it began to tire and I started to get some line back. There was one last run as it got closer and saw the boat. But after a struggle, I brought it in. The skipper grabbed the trace and steered the fish towards his mate who was ready with a large gaff.'

'Amazing!' Jake said.

'I can still remember being completely dazzled by the grey and silver colours of the fish, so much more startling close up. And the shark's pitch-black eyes.'

'How did you get it back to shore?' Jake asked.

'The skipper got two ropes, one of which he tied around the shark's head, just behind its pectoral fins, and the other around its tail. As soon as the fish was secure, he started the engine and moved in reverse for about half an hour.'

'Reverse?'

'Yes. That's how you drown a shark.'

Pete drew a worn photograph from a luxury leather wallet. There he was, standing next to a bloated shark hanging by its tail. Even in the pallor of death, with its own blood all over its teeth, the fish looked terrifying.

'And this relates to poker how?' Jake asked.

'Success comes to those who know when to slow play and when to accelerate,' Pete answered. 'If you get it right, there are peaks of pleasure waiting for you beyond your imagination. I've even been to Vegas.'

'When?'

'When I first won the national finals of the British Pub Championships.'

'You sound like you've won it more than once.'

'Just three times.'

As if to confirm that this was no fisherman's tale, two men who were heading for the poker table at the back of the pub paused on their way, shaking Pete by the hand and addressing him as 'the Mako'.

Pete turned back to Jake and smiled, baring his impeccably whitened teeth. 'My dream is to win the World Series of Poker in Vegas.'

Pete made as if to stand.

'Another whiskey?' Jake asked.

'Not for me. I only ever have one drink of alcohol before a game and then Diet Coke for the rest of the night.'

'Can I watch you play?'

'Of course.'

Jake followed Pete as he walked from the bar to an extension at the back of the pub. There was a table already set there with chips, guards, playing cards and buttons. It had a blue surface made of woven fabric.

When Pete entered the room, everyone stopped speaking. One man, clearly nervous, cast an imaginary line and pretended he was reeling Pete onto the table. Pete ignored him.

All the players showed signs of being intimated by Pete – all except one, a petite blonde in her early thirties whom the other players nicknamed the Man-Eater. She stared at the dealer. 'Get on with it,' she said.

And so, he did.

Pete sat and the man dealt the cards, beginning with a player on his left and going around the table until every player had two cards each.

Then the betting began.

Jake kept his eyes firmly fixed on every move Pete made. His friend gave nothing away. He sometimes ditched his cards, at other times he played, all the while speaking a new and unfamiliar language of 'calling' and 'checking', 'big blinds' and 'small blinds', 'raising' and 'drawing dead'.

The Mako turned on each player one by one.

After an hour, there were only five players left at the table.

After two hours, there were three.

And after three, there were just two – the Mako and the Man-Eater.

Jake knew enough about Pete's demeanour to see that he was giving his opponent respect. This woman was clearly no pushover. She had knocked out half the players herself.

For an hour, the two of them went head-to-head. First the Mako got the upper hand, gaining a big pot with 'Quads' – four of a kind. But then the Man-Eater pushed back, going all-in, risking her entire stack of chips on one hand. That hand turned out to be three Aces and two Kings – a 'Full House', beating Pete's two 'Pairs' (Queens and Tens).

With the balance of power shifting, the Man-Eater upped her aggression. Pete, however, kept calm, waiting for even the faintest trace of weakness. That finally came when the Man-Eater tried to bluff him. Pete smelt blood and went all-in. He had 'Trips' – three of a kind. She had nothing.

The game lasted two more hands.

The Man-Eater seemed deflated.

The Mako moved in.

For a moment, it seemed to Jake like his old friend was baring his teeth for the kill, his eyes rolling over in ecstasy. Pete won the woman's remaining chips with a pair of 'Hooks', or Jacks, followed by what Pete later confessed was 'a finely executed bluff'.

The game was over.

Pete had triumphed.

He had taken down nine players in just over four hours, the last of whom had proven a worthy adversary.

Jake watched as the dealer pushed a pirate's haul of coins and notes towards his friend.

As Pete left the table, he gave a tip to the dealer.

'How much did you win?' Jake asked.

'Three grand,' Pete replied. 'Not much, peanuts compared to what I can win in Vegas. But it's not bad for an evening's work.'

Jake frowned. Pete had won more money in one evening than he could hope to earn in an entire month.

'Can I ask you a favour?' Jake asked.

'Let me guess,' Pete chuckled. 'You want me to teach you how to play poker?'

Jake blushed.

Pete was laughing now. 'Don't be embarrassed. I feel like I owe you for going out with Sally while you were away, even if it was a very brief encounter. I'll teach you. Gladly.'

Jake smiled.

The two men went through the porch of the pub into the car park, where the rain was now pelting the tarmac.

'Meet me here same time next week,' Pete said.

With that, the two men shook hands and Pete drove off in his brand-new coupé. While Jake headed home in his rusting estate.

———

When Jake walked through his front door, Sally was still awake.

'Tommy missed you at bedtime,' she said as she kissed him on the cheek.

'I'm sorry. I decided to stop off at The Tempest for a pint and bumped into Pete Marley. Remember him?'

'I do,' Sally said. 'Tall, dark and handsome. Dated him briefly at school.'

'Yes, he told me,' Jake said.

Sally laughed. 'It was a long time ago. What's he doing now?'

'Works in the gaming industry.'

Jake hung up his coat, headed into the kitchen and began making himself a sandwich. Sally sat down while he sliced some 'no-thrills' luncheon meat.

'I've been doing some research while you've been out,' she said. 'I'm ready to take on some clients and I think I've found an agency. It'll supplement our income and help a bit with the mortgage.'

'It still won't be enough,' Jake said.

Jake sat down and started to nibble the corner of his sandwich. Sally reached across the worn tablecloth and placed her hand on his. Jake stared at her knuckles. Her hands were covered in red blushes and white blotches. They reminded Jake of the freckled meat in his sandwich.

'We may need to think outside the box,' Jake said, putting his sandwich down and covering it with a paper napkin.

'Do you see our lives as a box?' Sally asked, releasing her hand from his.

'Please don't analyse me,' Jake said. 'I'm just saying, maybe there are other things we could try, new income streams we haven't considered. It's not wise for us to depend so much on my job.'

'Why?' Sally asked. 'Is it in danger?'

Jake shook his head. 'I don't think so, but you never know.'

Sally got up and headed to the door. 'You're always down at this time of the year. Here,' she said, flicking on the main light, 'this'll help to brighten your spirits.'

That night Jake slept fitfully. He dreamed of poker games in pub annexes and casino ballrooms. He even dreamed of a heads-up tournament between himself and Pete.

The next morning, there was a new spring in his step as he went to work. Over the next seven days, he bought and devoured books and DVDs about poker. In dreary moments at his workplace desk, Jake fantasised about playing against the Man-Eater. On one occasion, the fantasy extended beyond the poker table to a hotel bar, where they stared into each other's eyes with a hungry longing.

On the third evening after meeting Pete, Jake typed 'internet poker' into the search engine of his home computer on the top floor of his home. He had just started to play when Sally walked in. He heard her soft footsteps just in time and managed to minimise the poker site.

'Just emailing the boss,' he sighed.

'That's okay. Come down when you're done and we can watch something funny on TV before going to bed.'

Jake mumbled and then logged onto his game again after Sally left.

For a moment, he winced that he had just lied to his wife, but the feeling of guilt decreased the more his winnings increased. When he eventually came downstairs, Sally was fast asleep on the sofa. It had not been two minutes; it had been over two hours. It was as if time had stood still.

Four days later, Pete strode into the bar of the King's Arms and Jake bought him a single malt. The two men carried their drinks into the back of the pub and sat in an alcove, leaning towards each other like secret lovers. A single candle flickered on the round, oak table.

'Ready?' Pete asked.

'Ready.'

'There are usually nine players at a poker table,' Pete began. 'In the first round, player 1 is given what's called the small blind and player 2 the big blind. If the small blind is £5 the big blind will always be double that.'

Pete sipped some whiskey.

'After the blinds are put into the pot, the dealer deals everyone two cards each, beginning with the two players who have put in the blinds. When everyone has their cards, the first round of betting begins. Some players will fold. Others will decide to play and make a bet. When the first round of betting has finished, the dealer places three cards face-up on the table.'

Pete drew three cards from a pack.

'This is known as the flop.'

'I've got a confession to make,' Jake said.

'What?'

'I've been playing a bit online since I last saw you.'

'Good. Well then, you'll know that the players who are left now look at the two cards they were dealt plus the three cards on the table and they decide whether to fold or to bet.'

'I've done both online,' Jake said.

'When this second round of betting has been completed, the dealer places a fourth card face-up for everyone to see. This card is known as the turn. At this point the remaining players have two cards in their hands and four cards on the table to make the best five card hand they can.'

Pete looked up and Jake nodded.

'Another round of betting begins and once again every remaining player has the choice to stay in and bet or to opt out by folding. Finally, if there are at least two players left at the table, the dealer places a fifth card face-up. This is known as the River Card. A last round of betting now happens. The winner is the player who can form the best five-card hand.'

Jake's eyes widened.

'And so, the process goes on and on until there's only one player left and that player wins all the money and goes home smiling.'

Jake took a gulp of ale as Pete continued.

'Now let's come to the actual five-card hands you can form. We'll start with the lowest. This is known as a high card hand. This is when all you've got is, say an Ace, with four other unrelated cards.'

'Happened to me last night,' Jake said.

Pete then reminded Jake of the other hands.

A Pair.

Three of a kind (Trips).

Five cards in a row (a Straight).

Five cards all of the same suit (a Flush).

Three cards the same suit and two cards the same suit (Full House).

Four of a kind (Quads).

Five cards in a row of the same suit (Straight Flush).

And the best hand of all, the unbeatable hand, a five-card hand with Ace, King, Queen, Jack and Ten in the same suit (the Royal Flush).

'There are two final things,' Pete said. 'First, reading your opponent. Let's have some fun.'

Pete dealt two cards face-down to Jake. Then he did the same for himself.

'Okay Jake, look at your cards.'

Jake picked up his two cards and looked at them, taking care to conceal them from Pete. In his hands, he held a Pair of Queens. As soon as he saw them he felt a tremor of excitement.

'You've got a high pair, haven't you? Either a Pair of Kings or a Pair of Queens,' Pete said.

'How did you know?'

Pete laughed. 'There were two telltale signs. The first was that your expression changed when you saw the hand. You need to develop a poker face, one that people can't read. The second, you didn't look at me when you put your cards on the table. That was a physical tell – a sign that you didn't want to let on that you had a good hand. After that, it was guesswork.'

'That's class,' Jake said.

'Reading your opponent is something you develop over time. But Jake, take time to observe the body language, the physical signals, that your opponents are transmitting.'

Jake nodded.

'One further thing,' Pete added. 'Always observe the betting patterns of your opponents and don't forget to weigh up probabilities.'

'Well, I teach maths,' Jake interjected.

'That's an advantage!' Pete laughed. 'And don't forget your position. Where you sit at the table is critical. Always remember, where you are in the order of play will determine your strategy. You can have the same hand in seats 3 and 9 but play them in a different way. And only time and experience can teach you that.'

There was a pause as the two men sat back in their chairs.

It was Jake who spoke first.

'Just as a matter of interest,' he said. 'Could you look at your two cards?'

Pete smiled, nodded, then lifted the cards to his face. He glanced at them before placing them face-down on the table.

'What do you think I've got?'

Just then Jake began to sense an old and familiar intuition. Since he was a child, he had possessed the ability to assess people's characters. His mother had seen it in him and told him that he had inherited it from her.

As Jake studied Pete, he knew his mentor was posturing.

'You've got nothing,' Jake said. 'I'm guessing a seven and a two.'

'Very impressive!' Pete exclaimed, turning his cards over to reveal a Seven of Spades and a Two of Hearts.

'I think I may have something of a gift when it comes to reading people,' Jake whispered.

'Well if that hand is anything to go by, then I agree.'

'Here,' Pete added, 'let's try some more hands.'

Pete shuffled the pack before setting two cards face-down in front of him. He turned the corners of both.

'What have I got?'

'You've got a Pair of Nines.'

Pete turned up his cards. 'That's phenomenal!'

For the next ten minutes, Pete kept dealing Pocket Cards and Jake kept outwitting him.

'This is what I saw in my dream,' Jake said after Pete conceded defeat.

'What dream?'

'A few nights ago, I saw myself beating you in a heads-up battle.'

'Are you psychic?' Pete asked.

'All I know is that I have this weird ability to read people and see things ahead of time in dreams.'

'Well, I can tell you two things right now,' Pete said. 'The first is that I'm never going to play you at poker!'

The two men laughed and lifted their glasses to cement their agreement.

'And the second?'

'The second is that this ability could mean you make more money than you could ever dream of.' Pete lowered his glass.

'In fact, let's try this gift out. How about I take you in the Merc to a cash game? You can play and I can watch.'

'Really?'

'There's a game a week on Monday at a bar forty miles from here. I'll pick you up from home at 7 p.m. What's your address?'

Jake typed the details into Pete's phone.

'Don't tell Sally what we're doing,' Jake said.

'Ah, okay. What's our story, then?'

'Old mates going out for a pint.'

'Right you are,' Pete said, tapping his nose.

—⁓—

The following Monday night, Jake heard the doorbell and he dashed down the stairs after freshening up in the bathroom.

'I'll get it,' he said.

But Sally was already at the door.

'Pete!' she exclaimed.

Pete took Sally by the shoulders and kissed her on both cheeks.

'Break it up!' Jake said, half laughing. 'Anyone would think you two are still dating.'

'Trust me,' Pete grinned. 'If we were still dating, I'd be a lot less formal.'

Jake winced.

Sally walked back into the kitchen while Jake poked his head into the sitting room. Billy was playing a campaign on his Xbox while his little brother Tommy was watching on, imitating the soldiers on the screen by making the sound of an AK-47.

'Bye boys.'

Billy grunted but Tommy jumped up, ran to his dad, threw his arms around his neck, and kissed him several times.

'Bye, Daddy.'

Jake turned towards the front door and as he did, he noted that the white paint was peeling around the porch and the door needed replacing. He stepped outside and climbed into Pete's silver Mercedes. As he turned to look back at his house, he saw a net curtain draw back into place, and wondered whether it had been Sally or the boys.

'Time to go,' Pete said.

No sooner had the two men climbed into the coupé than Pete put his foot down and the car accelerated to 70 mph. A journey that should have taken thirty minutes took half that time.

Arriving at the pub, Pete and Jake marched into the bar. Several people recognised Pete and nodded.

'What'll it be, champ?' the landlord asked.

'Two Cokes, Bill,' Pete answered.

Pete took the drinks and escorted Jake to a back room. There in the centre, underneath several suspended lights, was the same kind of poker table that Jake had seen in the King's Arms. Eight players were chatting and drinking at the table. A few spectators were seated in the shadowy fringes of the room. Several players thanked God loudly that Pete wasn't playing before Jake saw his seat, walked as nonchalantly as he could and took it. Somehow one of the legs of the chair became entangled in a piece of carpet and Jake stumbled, causing the £50 worth of chips in front of him to cascade across the table in an almost perfect vertical line towards the dealer.

'Bit early for all-in,' one player laughed.

Jake recovered his chips and his poise and the dealer got to work. He shuffled the cards and then passed every player two cards, starting on his left with the player next to him, before proceeding around the table. Jake was sitting in seat 8.

Jake observed what every player did. Player 3 folded, throwing his cards with disdain into the middle of the table. He was a working man with big forearms. As Jake observed him the word *impetuous* formed in his mind.

Player 4 put in the same amount as the big blind, £1. He was a skinny man in a creased black suit and a dark blue tie that had seen far better days. Jake noticed that the tie was stained in the middle with some food. *Nervous*, Jake thought.

Player 5 was a young man in his early twenties, wearing a baseball cap sideways. He was wearing a designer polo shirt and an expensive golden watch. Jake watched as he tapped his fingers on the table for a few seconds, keeping time to a song that was blaring out through an earphone whose black lead was visible underneath his black baseball cap. Player 5 folded and chewed gum. *Overconfident.*

Player 6 was a middle-aged woman with black hair in a bun, Audrey Hepburn style. She was plump, smiled a lot and had a small teddy bear – about six inches tall – sitting on her cards.

'Not this time Teddy,' she muttered, lifting the bear and folding her cards. *Deceptive.*

Player 7, on Jake's right, was a man in his fifties with beads of sweat on his brow. He quickly put £1 into the middle and as he did so, Jake read him. *Reckless.*

Now it was Jake's turn. He paused, breathing calmly, before turning up both his cards, covering them with his left hand, while almost peeling the top left corners with his right. As Jake lowered his head to look, he saw that he had a Pair of Eights, one Spade and one Club, known as The Dead Man's Hand. He carefully put the edges of both cards back on the table and sat upright, looking blankly ahead.

Jake remembered something Pete had taught him. 'It's all about position. If you get a middle pair when you're in an early or middle position on the table, be very careful. Good players often chuck those cards because they can get you into real trouble. But get a middle pair in a late position, you can bet aggressively if no one has done so before you.'

Jake moved his right hand to his stack of plastic chips. He took ten red ones, worth £10, and said, 'Call and raise', as he threw them between his fingers and thumb into the middle of the table.

Player 8, a woman in a business suit, white blouse and expensive rings and necklace, folded without hesitating. She reminded Jake of a magpie and he sensed the word *acquisitive.*

Now all nine players had made their move, either committing to the game or folding.

Jake took a deep breath.

The dealer turned to players 1 and 2, who had placed the small and big blinds respectively. Player 1 folded. Player 2 looked at Jake for a few moments. He had placed £1 into the middle with the big blind. He needed to put another nine £1 chips into the pot to continue. He folded. It was now player 7, with the greasy hair and the sweaty brow. He didn't waste a moment before he called and raised, matching Jake's £10 and putting a further £10 in £1 coins into the pot. Jake studied him as he did. He saw the desperation again in the man's eyes. He noticed an extra bead of sweat beginning to make its way down from his brow, now coloured by the dark grease from his hair.

Jake knew what he had to do. His heart was racing but his face was stony cold. 'All-in,' he said, pushing every chip of his £50 into the middle.

Pete grinned in the shadows.

Mr Reckless on Jake's right went as white as snow then mucked his cards into the middle of the table. Jake had outplayed him without resorting to his special gift. And he had won a hand before it had even got to the flop.

From then on, Jake began to play in the same clinical way he had seen from Pete. Sometimes he played tight and only bet when he had a strong hand. At other times, he played aggressively when he had a weak hand. Sometimes he fast-played a strong hand. At other times, he slow-played. Whatever he did, Jake worked hard to vary his game and to avoid playing with a consistent and unvaried pattern.

As player after player left – starting with Mr Reckless and the Magpie – Jake remained at the table.

The two players who had begun the game in seats 1 and 2 went. The man with the dirty tie and the man with the builder's arms followed.

Soon it was just Jake, the young man with the baseball cap and the woman with the teddy bear. Jake's stack was the lowest, £100. The woman had £120. The boy in the cap had £230, and he was the first of them to go after misreading the strength of the woman's cards and going all-in. He lost £120 in one hand and then the rest to Jake.

Now Jake was heads-up with the woman with the Audrey Hepburn hairdo. He had £210. She had £240. She was ahead, but Jake remembered Pete's golden rule of heads-up play – 'be aggressive'.

The first hand he was dealt was an Ace and a Ten of Clubs, not a bad hand for a heads-up situation. The small blind was now £10 and the big blind £20. The two players put their blinds in. Jake matched the big blind and raised £50.

The woman called. There was now £130 in the pot. The flop came down, 'Ace of Spades, Five of Clubs, Two of Clubs'. The woman bet £75 without delay. Jake, with two Aces, was in a strong but by no means unassailable position. With two Clubs in his hand and a further two Clubs on the table, he also had a chance of hitting a Flush – five cards of the same suit. Jake called, putting in £75.

There was now £280 in the pot.

The fourth card was dealt. It was a King of Hearts.

Jake thought for a moment. He believed his two Aces were still good and that if they weren't, there was still an 'out' with the Flush draw. He pushed in £100.

The woman called.

It was now time for the River Card.

The dealer, sensing the drama, seemed to take an eternity to place the fifth card face-up alongside the four community cards. It was the Three of Clubs. Jake had a Flush.

The woman went all-in.

Jake went all-in too.

She revealed her cards first. Trip Kings – a very good hand.

But Jake had a Flush.

In the final hand, the woman pushed all-in straight after receiving her Pocket Cards. Jake responded by matching her £30. She turned over a King of Hearts and a Three of Spades. Jake turned over a Six of Clubs and a Deuce of Diamonds. The flop came down – King of Diamonds, Eight of Spades, Six of Diamonds. Jake had a Pair of Sixes, but the woman had a Pair of Kings. She was ahead.

The fourth card came down, a Three of Hearts. Jake still had a Pair of Sixes, but his opponent now had two Pairs – Kings and Threes. She was now ahead and Jake was in trouble.

The River Card was dealt.

There was a gasp.

There on the table was the Six of Hearts.

The woman groaned.

She had two Pairs.

Jake had Trip Sixes.

'You can't play cards with the Devil,' she sighed, looking at the three Sixes on the table.

The small audience clapped.

The dealer pushed the £450 in chips towards Jake.

Jake gave him a tip.

The dealer nodded.

Jake shook the woman's hand. He then cupped the chips, took them to the bar, and redeemed them for cash.

Pete patted his friend on the back as he led him to his car. Neither uttered a word. They kept quiet until they reached the car park of the King's Arms, where Pete turned to Jake.

'You did really well tonight,' he said. 'You've learned very quickly that it's more important to play the player than the card. And you read other players perfectly.'

Jake nodded.

'But from now on, you're on your own, my friend.'

The following day, Jake decided it was time to take things to the next level. From then on, he began to play twice a week in a local pub. And he continued to win.

One evening, in a private cash game in a mock Tudor mansion, he won £20,000 and went out to buy a new car after work the next day. He drove it to the front door of his house, announcing in advance that there was a surprise coming at 6 p.m. When the shiny new vehicle arrived – a silver sports saloon, fuel-injected, with a branded and custom-designed interior – the boys went crazy and showed their father an adulation and appreciation that he'd not seen in a very long time, especially from his older son, Billy.

Sally, though, was a different matter.

'How can we afford that on our budget, Jake?'

'I paid for it in cash.'

'Where did you get the money from?'

Jake tapped his nose. 'That's my little secret, honey.'

'I don't like secrets. We've never had secrets before, Jake.' She stormed indoors.

For weeks Jake and Sally barely spoke, until things came to a head just as Christmas approached. One Monday evening in early December, Jake came home late. He had stayed on at work and played poker online, participating in a tournament in which, for once, none of his usual tactics had worked. In a desperate attempt to dig himself out of a hole, he had spent more and more cash until – with one last disastrous hand – he emptied the secret account where he banked his winnings. With nothing left, he had walked out of his office and driven home far too fast. He was stopped by a police officer and given an on-the-spot fine. When he arrived home, he was not his usual, poker-faced self, but a volcano on the point of eruption.

Sally sat down with him at the kitchen table. 'Sweetheart,' she said, 'what's wrong?'

'Nothing,' Jake replied, pulling away. 'I'm fine.'

'No, you're not. The one thing you're definitely not is fine.'

Jake stared at their ageing fridge.

'I know there's something wrong,' she continued. 'You've been different lately, staying after work for hours and hours. Then, when you do come home, you don't spend time like you used to with the boys. And you're sharp with them at bedtime. It's as if they can't get to sleep quick enough for you and, as soon as they are, you shut the door in the upstairs study and you're on that computer again.'

'I am not!'

'Yes, you are. And when I want to go to bed, we don't go together. You're typing away until the early hours. I'm worried about you.'

Jake turned towards his wife, changing both his look and his tone.

'I'm sorry, honey,' he said. 'I know I've been acting differently. But it's work. I've got a real chance of becoming vice-principal in the new year. I'm sorry if I've been short with you or the boys. I'm doing all this for them and I'm doing it for you.'

'Okay sweetie,' she said. 'Don't get me wrong, I appreciate all you do for the family, I really do. But I don't like what it's doing to you, to us. Please tell me this is only temporary.'

Jake took hold of Sally's arm, leaning his head on her shoulder. 'I promise,' he said.

Jake nestled into his wife, grateful for the calm he felt as her hand caressed his head.

But Jake realised he was in trouble. He had managed to get out of jail on the River but next time he might not be so lucky and she might not be so trusting. Hiding in Sally's embrace, he resolved to be even more careful.

For the next two weeks, he held off the poker. He came home on time from work and read to the boys after putting them to bed. He didn't go to his computer late at night or early in the morning. And he stayed home every evening.

Christmas was now fast approaching. It was mid-December and Jake wanted to spoil Sally and the boys. He had remembered Christmas Day a year ago when the family had opened their presents underneath the Christmas tree. They had been hard up and the gifts were modest. Jake had bought Sally an annual subscription to her favourite magazine and he had bartered for a second-hand Xbox game for Billy. He had found a plastic replica of a Second World War Tommy Gun for Tommy, joking that the weapon had been named especially after him. Sally had been grateful. Billy had grunted that the game wasn't new and didn't have the instructions. Only Tommy seemed happy. He spent much of the holiday running in and out of every room in the house, peering out of windows, shooting imaginary enemies. In the end, the noise had annoyed everyone, including Jake.

This year, Jake was determined they would do better. His marriage was sailing perilously close to the rocks, he knew that, so he decided that he wanted to splash out and buy Sally a golden eternity ring he'd found in a catalogue that had dropped through their letter box, while he was at home being responsible. In the same catalogue, he had also found watches for the boys – limited edition silver ones, branded with the colours and the images of their favourite comic book heroes. Billy's was a Batman watch. Tommy's was festooned with Spiderman motifs. He ordered the gifts on his credit card and when they arrived, Jake looked to see if the appealing photos in the thick catalogue had done them justice. They had.

'Now to pay for these,' he thought.

Jake knew what to do. One evening, two days before Christmas Eve, he braved the falling snow and drove his new car to a pub twenty miles away. He told Sally that he was going to the nearest mall to do some last minute, late night Christmas shopping, and she believed him.

In fact, he was heading to a private, backroom poker game.

Pete had often told him that poker players become great because they are prepared to risk losing their stack, not because they hold on tenaciously to every chip. So, he resolved to play aggressively that night. About an hour later, Jake was sitting at a table in a well-lit room and was starting to read his opponents.

As Christmas songs played in the background, Jake got to work. Carols came and went, and so did the poker players, until only Jake and a suited business man from the City were left. He was sharp, but not sharp enough. Jake listened to the words of a carol as he prepared the coup de grâce.

What can I give him, poor as I am?
If I were a shepherd, I would give a lamb.
If I were a rich man, I would play my part
What I can I give him, I give my heart.

As the verse disappeared, Jake struck like a frenzied predator and pocketed two grand's worth of winnings. He gave £200 in chips to the dealer, adding 'Merry Christmas', before receiving his winnings at the bar – £1,800 in a tight roll of bank notes, held together by two large plastic bands.

Jake fondled the bank roll in his raincoat pocket as he walked to the car, keeping a careful lookout for anyone who might want to rob him of his night's winnings. He drove home through the snow, humming the melodies of the carols he had heard.

When he arrived, Sally was still awake and waiting for him. 'How did you get on, darling?' she asked.

Jake had wrapped the two watches as well as Sally's ring (resting on a velvet bed inside a felted, dark blue gift box).

'Very successful,' Jake answered, revealing the gifts wrapped in white paper adorned with dancing Santas.

'Oh sweetheart,' Sally said.

Jake led his wife upstairs to the bedroom and dimmed the lights. He kissed her face tenderly, before locking onto her lips.

For an hour Jake lost himself within his wife's embrace, like a boy immersing himself in the warm waves of a faraway ocean.

And then sleep swept him away, the deepest sleep Jake had enjoyed in a long, long time.

The following morning, Jake was not as careful as he normally was. Before he drove to his bank to deposit £1,000, he took the remaining money and simply left it on the desk of the upstairs study with a receipt from the pub. It was only as he drove home after completing his banking that Jake realised his mistake. He hadn't put the cash or the paperwork in the usual hiding place – a safety deposit box on the top shelf of a wardrobe in the study. He wasn't to know that Sally would be cleaning the house from top to bottom for the Christmas holidays, starting with the study. He wasn't to know that Sally was already dusting the desk and wiping the screen of the computer. And he wasn't to know that she now had the receipt in her hand, wet from her crying.

Jake raced back to the house, unlocked the front door, and ran upstairs.

As he entered the study, Sally was sitting on the floor with her back to the wall, her face red with tears. As she saw Jake enter, her chest began to heave, her sobs returned. She simply lifted the banknotes towards him.

'You lied.'

Jake took the notes from her hand and put them on the desk. He tried to kiss her, but Sally got up and walked out of the room, throwing the tear-stained receipt at her husband's feet as she did. For the rest of the day, Sally wouldn't speak to him. She kept herself busy dusting – furiously dusting – everything that needed dusting and a lot of things that didn't. The only time he heard her talk was when she spoke to the boys, which she did with tenderness. But then, at bedtime, Sally went downstairs and slept on the sofa, taking her two pillows and a grey Christmas blanket covered in red reindeers.

She couldn't sleep that night and nor could he. When the morning of Christmas Eve arrived, their tiredness now compounded the tension between them. Sally came upstairs and went through the bathroom first. Jake followed, hoping to wash off his guilt in the hot jets of water from the ageing shower head. But as the minutes went on, his guilt turned to grief and then his grief to anger – an anger that had been suppressed for decades but was now on the point of eruption.

'Why did I ever marry her?' he thought.

Having dried and dressed himself, he seized the bank roll from the study desk and thrust it in his pocket. As he walked downstairs, he decided that he would spend the day at work. It was Christmas Eve and technically the holidays, but Jake needed to hide and his office at the college was as good a place as any to take cover from the barrage of blame.

He stepped into the paint-peeling hall of his house and put on his raincoat, placing the car keys to his silver sports saloon in his pocket before striding into the kitchen. By the time he opened the kitchen door, he was at boiling point.

Sally rose, her face blanched and devoid of make-up, and stood at the kitchen table. The boys had already come downstairs in the excitement of their festive anticipation and were in their dressing gowns eating their favourite cereals, having an animated discussion about what their 'big present' was going to be this Christmas.

Sally spoke first.

'Jake, I'm just going to say this once and I want you to hear it. There are some things I will tolerate but there are others that I won't. And I won't tolerate becoming your caretaker and these boys will not become the victims of your compulsion. You need to sort yourself out.'

'No, you need to sort yourself out!' Jake shouted. 'I've had enough of you speaking to me like this.'

Sally looked at him. At first she looked shocked by the appearance and strength of his emotions, but then her face became set like flint.

'Jake, I am not and can never be your mother!' she said.

'Don't give me that rubbish,' Jake shouted. 'It's got nothing to do with that.'

'Then what has it got to do with?'

'I'm doing all this for you, for us.'

'You're doing this for yourself,' Sally said, 'to mask the pain.'

'What pain?'

'Abandonment.'

Jake felt momentarily unbalanced, like a skittle teetering

between falling and standing. Then he recovered his poise and spoke. 'It's got nothing to do with that.'

'Then what?'

Jake's voice was getting louder now. 'I'm bored. I'm bored with life. And… I'm bored with you.'

Jake's voice was now so forceful that he failed to hear the rising crescendo of little Tommy's crying.

Finally, Billy yelled, 'Leave Mum alone!'

'I'll leave her alone, all right!' Jake shouted. And with that he reached inside his coat pocket, drew out the smaller packet of the three, and hurled it on the kitchen floor.

He turned, marched to the front door, opened it, shut it, walked to his car, slammed another door, fired up the engine. He turned to look back through the frosted glass of his car window. He saw an upstairs curtain opening and Sally's face pressed against the pane, mouthing two words.

'Please, Jake.'

But Jake ignored her.

Downstairs, the front door opened, and Tommy stepped out. His favourite teddy bear was hanging from his left hand and his right hand was wiping a tear from his eye. He was trying to say something, but the words had got stuck like a fishbone in his throat.

Jake faltered before his anger once again engulfed him. He pushed his foot to the floor and accelerated out of the driveway onto the icy street.

As the snow began to fall, he raced through the village and across the railway bridge out towards the motorway.

In no time, Jake was in the fast lane with no map, no destination, and no compass.

He had made his decision.

It was Christmas Eve, and it was the worst decision of his life.

Daddy,

*It's Chrissmas Day morning and there's no pressie from u
under the Chrissmas tree
But the only pressie I want is u, any way
So I dont care bout that
Last nite I went into the study and fetched yore favrite coat
from the wardrobe – the one u only ware at very speshal
times
I put it on my bed and hugged it tite all nite, just to be close
to u
But its not the same.
Its like Chrissmas paper without a pressie inside
Today I played Xbox alot
And also looked out the window upstairs in my room to see
if u came home yet
But yore car is still gone
There's lots of snow so maybe you cant drive
I hope u r not in truble, Daddy
There are so many horrid peeple
If u want to U can borrow my Tommy gun – it will keep u
safe if peeple try to hurt u
I wish u wood come home, even if u have to wark thru the
snow
Chrissmas is rubbish without u
Mummy is crying all the time and Billy keeps sayin he hates u
But I dont hate u
I miss u
I miss playin shootin games round the house with u*

I miss u splashin me at bath time and readin stories at bed time
I miss u so mutch
Please come back soon, Daddy
I will hug yore coat til i can hug u
Happy Chrissmas Daddy
Wherever u r
I luv u

Tommy, like the gun
xxxxx

2. The Priest

It was over an hour before Jake was aware of the throbbing in his hands. It was only when he nearly bumped the back of a family car, full of excited children and bulging bags, that he had disengaged his internal autopilot.

'Damn it!' he shouted, startled by the sound of his voice.

Jake now became aware of the pain in his hands and wrists. He had been channelling all his rage into the tanned brown leather trim of his steering wheel and his hands were sore and sweaty from the intensity of their clawing. He slowed down, waiting for the next motorway sign to pinpoint his position. As he passed colossal articulated trucks making their final journeys before Christmas, he peered between each one to look for telltale boards with locations on them. After several minutes, he saw one in the distance, its blue painted background even more striking against the light snow lying on the banks and hedgerows beside the carriageway.

Jake gasped. He had travelled nearly 100 miles in just over an hour.

He decreased the rate of his breathing and began to feel into the pockets of his raincoat, keeping one hand on the wheel. He felt the shapes of the two wrapped boxes with the watches he had planned to give his boys and sensed a sting of regret, but this soon subsided when he recognised the contours of the rolled-up bank notes, £800 of them. This was the buy-in to his new life of freedom. He would head to the north, to a city that he had read about online – a city with glittering new casinos by the river and sleek and shiny hotels jostling for a player's patronage nearby. This was where he would begin to build a new life – he called it 'Casino City'.

Jake settled into the fast lane once again and thought through his strategy. All he had were the clothes he was wearing, so he would need to stop at a motorway services. Then, having bought some clothes and toiletries, he would drive towards the bright lights, check in to a hotel and start playing cash games straightaway.

Within minutes, Jake found himself rifling through a display of shirts in a motorway store. He bought three – one pink, one light green and one blue with white stripes (the only one he deemed half-decent). Concerned about the cold, he grabbed the last remaining grey hoodie off a stubborn coat hanger. He added socks and boxer shorts and went to pay, turning his face away from the tasteless colours of his items as a young woman – with a Christmas hat and a distant stare – processed his sale.

Next, he dropped into a pharmacy and bought the only set of men's travel toiletries left on sale. It was a Christmas gift box which contained a 50 ml bottle of eau de toilette, a razor with the customary promise of "longer-lasting blades", a shaving brush, a toothbrush, toothpaste, shower gel and some shaving cream (pretentiously spelt crème, Jake thought), with a lather that claimed to produce maximum slipping and minimum drying – all this in a zip bag in imitation brown leather, standing in a package with decorated trees carrying gaudily coloured lights.

Leaving the shop, Jake returned to his car and filled up with fuel. He bought a large latte, extra shot with gingerbread syrup, before rejoining the motorway.

'Three hours to freedom,' he thought, as he pressed down on the accelerator and manoeuvred into the fast lane.

The further north he went, the heavier the snow was falling. By the time Jake joined the main road leading to Casino City, the conditions were ideal for a white Christmas but awful for driving.

As Jake saw the city lights he passed under the huge wingspan of an angel, a steel sculpture of a celestial being that watched over the passing drivers, tilting forward slightly to create the impression of an imminent embrace. He made his way over a steel bridge towards the riverside of the city where the casinos would compete for his custom.

Jake decided to check into a hotel within walking distance from a casino which had caught his eye and whose façade was throbbing with bright lights in the early evening darkness. Jake could make out the words 'Blackjack', 'Roulette', 'Slots' and 'Poker' in large luminescent, white strobes on the facade of what looked like a new, purpose-built palace. Other words, like 'Late Bar' and 'Restaurant' glowed beneath them in the gathering gloom.

He drove into the hotel car park and made his way to the reception.

'Merry Christmas,' said the young man behind the desk.

Jake ignored the greeting. The moment he had seen the man, he had read him. Fake. But then, who was he to judge on that score?

'Any rooms?'

'I'll just check for you, sir.'

The man moved to a computer and began to type onto the keyboard. 'We have a standard room with a king-size bed.'

'How much?'

'£120 a night, sir.'

'Okay,' Jake replied, after making momentary calculations in his head. 'I'll pay you in cash for three nights.'

'That's against hotel policy, sir. We need a credit card in case you use the mini bar in your room or order room service.'

'I'll not be using those,' Jake said. 'I just want a room to sleep in. I'll always make sure my bills are paid in advance, but it'll have to be in cash. I don't have a credit card on me.'

Jake was lying. He had one in his back trouser pocket but he had no intention of using it in case his location was traced.

'Let me consult with the manager, sir,' the receptionist said, sloping into a room behind the counter, emerging a few minutes later with a tall, dark-haired man in a well-tailored suit. Jake sensed one word. Safety.

'Good evening, sir. You'd like to pay your bills in cash?'

'That's right. I will always pay my bills a week in advance and I'll pay them in full. If you're not happy at any point with this arrangement, I will understand if you want to terminate it and ask me to move to another hotel.'

Whether it was the threat of taking his patronage elsewhere, or the polite way in which he spoke, the manager warmed to Jake and invited him to sit with him on a sofa in the foyer. Jake perched just beneath the branches of a Christmas tree. The manager sat a few metres away in an armchair. The man was in his late fifties. He had a full head of dark brown hair, but the sides had flecks of grey and his skin was creased. He had a professional

38

demeanour about him which sat well with his tastefully chosen shirt and his freshly pressed suit. He was a man who took care over his appearance.

'My name's Tom,' he said, reaching out his hand.

Jake took it and replied without thinking, 'I have a son called Tom.'

'Are you in trouble?' the manager asked.

'I'm just here to play the casinos.'

Tom paused, took one more look at Jake, then glanced at the Christmas lights above the new visitor's head.

'I'm not quite sure why, but I'm going to make an exception. Pay your bill a week in advance every week, starting from next Monday. You've paid up till then but on Monday morning I'd like you to pay for the week in full and to continue doing that. Does that sound reasonable?'

'It is. Thank you.'

'It's my pleasure, sir,' Tom replied, 'Happy Christmas.'

With that he got up, walked back to the reception desk, informed the clerk of the arrangement and instructed him to enter details into the hotel's system. Jake handed over £360 in crisp banknotes, received two plastic hotel keys and took the elevator to the fourth floor. From there it was only a very short walk to room 444.

'Hmmm, Trip Fours,' he chuckled. 'Not a bad hand.'

Jake opened the door and entered a spacious room with an en suite bathroom, a large bed with a set of purple cushions (which Jake immediately swept onto the floor) and a desk with a lamp.

He went to the windows and peered through the net curtains at the coloured, flashing lights of the casinos by the river. They seemed warm and welcoming, almost to be winking at him. He then drew the big blinds and sat on his bed, appreciating the comfort of its mattress. He looked at the large television standing on a fake mahogany dresser.

'No time for that,' he thought, jumping to his feet.

Pulling his grey hoodie over his torso, he left one key in a slot next to the door before walking down the corridor, pausing to check that his door had shut behind him. He made his way via the elevator to the ground floor, nodded to Tom in the foyer as he left the hotel, and strode along the riverside past park benches towards the first casino.

It was now snowing hard and Jake's shoes and socks were becoming damp in the slush. Borne on by his unstoppable intent, he barely noticed. His mind was focused on his first ever experience of casino culture and his heart was swelling with anticipation. As soon as he entered through the well-lit entrance, he headed past several strapping bouncers in black suits to the reception desk where he enquired about their poker facilities. A young, ginger-haired woman with freckled hands gave him his directions.

'The poker room's at the back of the hall upstairs. Tonight, it's a special Christmas Eve tournament. Normally I'd ask you to go through a registration process, but someone had to drop out so there's a spare seat at table seven. The tournament starts in twenty minutes and runs from 7 p.m. until midnight. The buy in is £50 and the winners at the final table share £5,000. There's a registration fee of £5.'

'I'll take the seat,' Jake said.

He took out his bank notes and paid the girl.

'You'll get £50 worth of chips from the dealer at your table,' she said.

Jake collected his ticket with the table and seat number and stepped onto the escalator. When he reached the top, there were slot machines and tables positioned under dangling copper lights and enormous chandeliers. Hundreds of people were playing, some sitting at machines which chirped and chirruped, flashed and glowed, others standing at tables, placing bets at Roulette and Blackjack.

Jake stopped behind a middle-aged lady who was sitting at a terminal and playing games with exotic names full of Eastern promise – *The Book of Ra* and *Pharaoh's Fortune*. Every so often, an alluring statement would appear as if by magic in front of her: 'Win Free Spins in the Mystical Bonus!' Jake had no idea what this meant but he sensed the woman did, as her hands moved with the speed and precision of a concert pianist around the flashing buttons at the base of the screen in front of her.

Jake left the bleeping and chiming of her machine and headed towards the tables. The first one had a Roulette wheel. Jake watched as a man with a scruffy beard, smart jeans, leather jacket and suede shoes took a £20 note out of his pocket. Within ten minutes, he had built a small stack of chips.

Jake glanced at his watch. 6.58 p.m. It was time to head to the poker room. He found a section of the floor cordoned off by a glass partition. Beyond it was the brave new world that Jake so craved – a richly carpeted space with twelve poker tables and nearly one hundred poker players primed to play. Before he entered, Jake drew the grey hood over his head and, grasping the toggles, tightened the garment into a cowl.

Jake made his way around the room and found his seat. As he sat down, one of the players observed his hoodie. He called him 'the Monk', a name that everyone at the table, and indeed the casino, used from then on.

A dealer in a baggy waistcoat leant towards Jake and said, '£50 in chips for you, sir.' She used her hands like a snow plough to shovel his new stack towards him.

Jake hugged his counters with both arms. These were not like the chips he was used to in the pub poker games. These were made of ceramic material and had their value printed on them. They made a brighter, lighter sound when Jake rattled them between his fingers. *This is the real deal*, Jake thought.

Jake conducted one more sweep around the table before the pit boss announced that mobile phones must now be switched off, that the only language spoken at the tables was to be English, and that the dealers could now shuffle up and deal. He rounded all this off with the words, 'Good luck and Godspeed.'

As he observed the other eight players, Jake tried to distinguish who around the table was there for entertainment betting and who was there for professional betting. He decided that only one opponent was probably a professional better – a cowboy in a beige suit. He looked like he knew what he was about, and Jake guessed that he was playing in all the casinos in the city, picking up enough money here and there to enjoy a comfortable if not luxurious Christmas. He also speculated – rightly, as it turned out – that the man had a huge Stetson, but that he had taken it off on entering the casino to respect the 'no hats' house rule.

Jake reached into his pocket and fetched his card guard. It was made of metal and painted in three colours – gold, black and white. It was designed in three sections. One third was painted gold and had a picture of black poker chip on it. The word CHIP was engraved against a white background on the circumference of the coin. The next third was painted in black and had a picture of a golden poker player's seat on it. The word CHAIR was engraved in white on the edge of the coin. The final third was painted in white and had a picture of a golden Cross on it with the word PRAYER engraved in gold against a jet-black background on the periphery.

Jake stared for a moment at the word 'prayer'. 'If there's anybody up there, I'd really appreciate some help tonight,' he said to himself.

Jake noticed two machines on the table designed to shuffle the cards mechanically rather than manually. He also spotted a 50-inch, super thin television screen on two of the walls in the room. They had digital clocks which counted down to the moment when the blinds had to change.

The dealer began passing two cards one by one to every player. Jake was left of the player who had put in the big blind – two £1 chips. He turned up the left-hand corners of both his cards. He had an Ace and a Ten of Hearts. He decided to call the big blind, casually and gently tossing two £1 chips into the centre of the table.

Now he turned his attention to the other players. On his left was a man in his fifties. As he turned up his cards, he chucked them with disdain into the centre of the table saying, 'I fold.'

The next player was a young woman in her thirties, dressed in a black blouse and skirt, with inky black hair and eyelashes. She turned her cards up, blinked several times and also folded.

Next was a man in his twenties, wearing a pair of sunglasses. As the man turned the corner of his cards he looked at them, put them back face-down as they had been, placed his card guard over them and paused. He put £5 into the pot, equalling the big blind but raising it by £3.

This player knew what he was doing, in stark contrast to the plump, red-faced man next to him. He was clearly a novice. He even cast a nervous look towards the dealer as if to make sure it was really his turn to play. He looked at his cards by drawing them to his chest, looked down (revealing a large double chin in the process), and frowned. He placed the cards down on the table and then slowly counted out five £1 chips and put them in the pot.

Player number 7 was a man in his seventies. He looked at his cards, then threw them into the middle. Players 8 and 9 did the same.

So now it was up to players 1 and 2, who had placed the small and big blinds. Player 1 decided not to continue. Player 2 put in £3 in £1 chips, protecting his big blind.

There were four players in the game.

The dealer turned a card face-down before revealing the flop – an Eight of Hearts, a Ten of Clubs, and a King of Hearts. Jake felt a rising tide of excitement. Not only did he have a Pair of Tens, he also had four Hearts in his hand. By the time the dealer dealt the River Card there were just two players left, Jake and the man in the sunglasses, and there was a sizeable pot to plunder.

As the River Card was dealt, Jake registered no emotion. It was a Jack of Hearts.

He had a Flush. Now all he had to do was calculate the odds that his opponent had a better hand.

The five cards on the table were the Eight of Hearts, Ten of Clubs, King of Hearts, Three of Spades and a Jack of Hearts. Jake thought through every possible permutation and probability and concluded he had the best hand. He placed £20 in four £5 chips into the centre of the table. His opponent called. Jake held his breath.

The man in the shades now put his cards face-up, with a smug grin on his face. He had a Queen and a Deuce of Hearts – making a Flush. But Jake's hand was stronger. He also had a Flush, but his had the highest card – the Ace of Hearts.

Jake paused before revealing his hand.

His opponent threw his arms up in dismay.

Other players at the table muttered. Once again Lady Luck was smiling on him.

And she continued to smile. In fact, she began to laugh as Jake swept his opponents aside with ease. Some of it was down to good reads, brilliant calculations and skilful play, but a lot of it was down to luck. In fact, Jake could never remember being so lucky.

It felt like no time at all before Jake was at the final table, seating the last nine players in the Christmas Eve tournament. Everyone at this table would win a cash prize, but Jake was after the £3,000. That would amount to a month's hotel bills, new clothes, plus good food – all from one night's work. It would be a firm foundation on which to build his new life.

Jake paused, as he always did, to slow his heart rate. As he relaxed, a young woman in casino uniform, who had been waiting on some of the other tables up until now, came up behind him, tapped him on the shoulder, and whispered in his ear, asking him if he would like a drink. Jake turned and noted that her pupils dilated as their faces almost touched. He could smell the scent on her neck and the aroma of her dark brown, shoulder-length hair. As he looked at her, he saw the word *Angel*.

He reached out his right hand and held her left arm, sensing a frisson of pleasure as their bodies met.

'I'll have a Diet Coke, please,' he said.

'Do you want ice and lemon with that, sir?'

Jake nodded before taking one more look at her brown eyes and turning back to the table. A few minutes later, the tall and slender valet returned with a small table on a wheeled trolley bearing his drink. She received his thanks, his money, his tip and his smile with a glow in her eyes.

'If there's anything more I can do for you, sir, please don't hesitate to say,' she said, smiling again.

'That's very kind, Sandra,' Jake replied, looking at the name badge pinned to her waistcoat just above her chest.

'I'll keep an eye out for you throughout the evening,' she said.

'In that case, let me give you this,' and with that Jake drew a £10 note out of his roll of remaining banknotes and placed it in the palm of Sandra's outstretched hand.

'Thank you, sir.'

Jake took a sip of his Coke before turning to the illuminated table and his opponents. He studied the other players and engaged in his customary practice of nicknaming them all.

Player 1: the Driver – a tall, muscular man with huge, tattooed arms and sensitive eyes.

Player 2: the Vampire – a thin, dark-haired woman with long, sharp fingernails and a flowing black dress.

Player 3: the Slicker – a young man in a pinstriped suit with wavy fair hair and blue eyes.

Player 4: the Big Mouth – a loud, overweight man in his forties who was obviously a bully.

Player 5: the Playboy – a young man in his early thirties with sunglasses, greased-back hair and an open shirt.

Player 6: the Boffin – a bespectacled woman with ragged hair and an intensely studious stare.

Player 7: the General – a late middle-aged man with a tweed jacket and impressive whiskers.

Player 8: the Assassin – an elegant woman in her forties in a sharp trouser suit.

As the pit boss walked to the table, Jake guessed the man was sixty years old – maybe a little younger – about six feet tall, and noticed that he was handsome and in good shape for his age. Jake saw one word. *Kindness.*

'Evening, Father Jim,' the tattooed player next to Jake said.

'Evening, big lad,' the pit boss replied in an Irish accent.

He now had the attention of all the players.

'This is the final table. Same rules apply. Good luck and Godspeed.'

Father Jim nodded at the dealer and the first cards were dealt. Over the next two hours the blinds increased more quickly than they had before, until only four players were left – Jake, the Boffin, the Driver and the Assassin.

The Boffin was knocked out first.

The Assassin was next to go. She went all-in before the flop after Jake had folded, trying in the process to push the Driver off her hand and pick up the blinds cheaply. But he called her and then revealed that he had a Pair of Kings. She had a Pair of Eights. The dealer placed three cards face-up on the table – a Deuce, a Five and an Eight. The Assassin licked her lips, readying herself for the kill. Fourth Street (the fourth card on the table) turned out to be a Jack – no good to either player. The River Card was turned to reveal the King of Spades. The Assassin swore. The Driver grinned. He had three Kings.

Out of the original 100 players, it was now only Jake and the Driver left. One of them would win £1,000 (second prize) and the other £3,000 (first prize) and a trophy.

A female valet now appeared, carrying a silver case with £3,000 in crisp, brand new £20 notes. She placed it on the table, posing and smiling as she did to no one in particular. Rows of chairs were set up near the final table, so that the two players could be watched side-on by a growing crowd.

Amidst the commotion, Sandra reappeared behind Jake's shoulder and asked if he needed anything. She stressed the word *anything*.

Jake had noticed that several of the men playing at the final table had paid girls to rub their heads, necks and shoulders while they played.

'The massage,' Jake said. 'How much is it?'

'£20 for five minutes, sir.'

Jake drew a note from his pocket. 'Go easy with me,' he said. Sandra laughed and then stood behind Jake, her flat stomach pressing close to the upright support of his chair, her chest to the top of his back. For the next ten minutes, Jake found himself in an unfamiliar place of serenity. As Sandra kneaded him with her strong, long and tender fingers, Jake allowed his tired mind to wander to a borderland between waking and sleeping.

Not even the glinting treasure chest full of bank notes, sitting a matter of inches away from his hands, could pull him out of his reverie and bring him back to consciousness. It was only when Father Jim took hold of a microphone, announced the names of the two players and wished them good luck and Godspeed that Jake came around and refocussed. Sandra lifted her hands from Jake's shoulders and disappeared into the background. Jake looked at the Driver. The Driver stared back. The two men stood and shook hands – Jake wincing as he felt the strength of the Driver's powerful grip. And then the final heads-up battle began.

For half an hour, the two men tried to outwit each other until, with two big wins, Jake became the overwhelming chip leader. In the final hand, the Driver pushed all his chips in on a strong hand – two Pairs, Aces and Queens – but Jake had a Full House – three Tens and two Fours.

When Jake revealed his hand the Driver sighed, then smiled and shook Jake's hand.

'I suppose it's right for a monk to win at Christmas,' he said, before drifting away as casino staff and spectators gathered round the Christmas Eve champion and applauded him.

Jake had never felt anything like it. The sense of approval, of affirmation, was as powerful as an anaesthetic, numbing the shame in his heart, relieving the pain. More than the money, it was the applause that soothed his soul. It helped him to forget the anger he felt towards those in his life who had not only done cruel things to him, but not done kind things for him. For a moment, the anaesthesia had led to amnesia, and Jake was hooked.

Jake received the treasure chest with £3,000 in cash and a small, especially engraved trophy with the words 'Christmas Eve' clearly written on its crystal façade. He lifted the trophy above his head and grinned from ear to ear.

Just as he was about to leave, Father Jim announced that it was almost Christmas Day and that the bars were open until midnight. Then he added, 'On behalf of all the staff, I want to wish you a very, merry Christmas. Good luck and Godspeed.'

With that, the thirty or forty people who had stayed began to circulate around the room, shaking each other's hands, wishing each other Christmas greetings.

Father Jim came up to Jake.

'Congratulations,' he said. 'Was that your first win?'

'It was my first time in a casino,' Jake replied, 'but not my first win. All I've been used to up until tonight is pub games. This is fantastic. This is the nuts.'

'Well,' Father Jim replied, 'you clearly have beginner's luck.'

'Lucky in cards, unlucky in life,' Jake said.

'I'm sorry to hear that. Let's hope you don't get unlucky with cards as well.'

'I don't think there's any chance of that. I've got a gift for this.'

Father Jim smiled. 'Listen,' he said, 'why don't you come with me to the bar for a pint of the black stuff on me?'

'What's that?'

'Ach, it's Guinness – whose very existence is proof that God loves us.'

Jake said, 'First time for everything.'

Father Jim walked with Jake to the escalators and the two men descended to the ground floor to one of the bars.

'My usual and a pint of the black stuff, when you're ready.'

'Sure thing, Father Jim,' the barman replied. And within a minute there were two glasses on the bar, one with whiskey in it, and the other with a dark stout topped by a creamy lather.

They took their drinks in their hands and sat down. 'Here's to a very merry Christmas,' Father Jim said, raising his glass to Jake's.

'Is that whiskey?' Jake enquired, raising his.

'Irish best. I have one of these an evening. Any more than that and I'd be half-cut!'

'You like your whiskey, then?'

'Aye, I do. God invented whiskey to prevent the Irish from ruling the world!'

Jake chuckled.

'It's a perfect nightcap,' Father Jim said. And then, holding his glass up to the light, he added, 'Look at that, would you? Liquid gold! It's the glory of God in a glass, so it is!'

The two men paused to sip their drinks, Jake taking a small taste of his Guinness to begin with, before taking several large gulps as he began to appreciate the smooth, velvety taste.

'I see you like it,' said his companion.

'It's not bad,' Jake replied. 'Not bad at all.'

'I thought you might enjoy it.' Then, taking a larger sip of his own drink, Father Jim added, 'It's like a wee, torch-lit procession going down my throat!'

As he said this, Sandra walked past their table, casting a cursory but friendly glance towards Jake as she did. Father Jim, noticing the interaction, reached over the table when Sandra was out of sight and whispered, 'That's a fine-looking woman, to be sure.'

'She's beautiful,' Jake agreed, 'and tall.'

'Aye, she is that.'

The two men paused. Jake was the first to pipe up. 'May I ask you a personal question?'

'You may.'

'Why does everyone around here call you Father Jim? Are you a priest or something?'

Jake's companion put his glass of whiskey on the table. 'It's a long story, Jake.'

'I'm not going anywhere,' Jake said.

'I used to be a priest. I was ordained thirty-five years ago and spent many happy years serving the people of this city. Then I met a beautiful, unmarried woman in the Philippines. I was on a trip there to visit an orphanage my church had been supporting and there she was, helping the children. I had never set my eyes on anyone as stunning as her. I fell in love in an instant. All my years of resisting temptation seemed to count for nothing at that moment. And you know what?'

'What?' Jake replied.

'It wasn't just that I couldn't resist my feelings. I didn't want to.'

'Why would you?' Jake asked.

'As a priest, I was always taught that God's Son was single and that a priest is supposed to be single, too. I took a vow of chastity and spent my ordained life completely available to my people. Twenty-four hours a day.'

Jake nodded.

'For over three decades I was married to the Church. And I was happy in it, too. I loved the fraternity – the brotherhood of priests – to which I belonged. I loved being at the centre of the

Catholic community in the parishes I served. Ach, they were a family to me. But when I met Gloria…'

'What happened?'

'She and I fell head over heels in love, that's what happened. We were both single. She was in her forties and had been waiting faithfully for the right man all her life. I was in my fifties and I found the love of my life – when I wasn't looking.'

'I bet that caused complications.'

'Aye, it did. At first my parish saw nothing amiss in my visits to the Philippines. They assumed that my heart had expanded with mercy for the poor and, in a sense, it had. These were Gloria's people and, because I'd fallen in love with her, I'd fallen in love with them. But the truth was my heart had expanded with love for Gloria and the more my heart ignited, the more my desire for her grew with it. I didn't just love her, I really wanted her. And the fire that began to grow in me felt unstoppable. I was aching for her all the time.'

'Sounds normal,' Jake said.

'It wasn't long before Gloria and I realised that we were at a crossroads. Either we gave up our relationship or I gave up my life as a priest. After many tears, we decided to get married.'

'What did you do?' Jake asked.

'First of all, I went to my bishop. He told me I was away in the head, but I replied that I had never been so at home in my head or in my heart and that I wanted to marry her. Eventually he could see that I was not going to back down, so he told me that I'd have to be laicised.'

'Laicised?'

'Oh sorry, forgive me. You're not Catholic, are you?'

'No, I'm not really religious.'

'Nor am I,' Father Jim laughed. 'I prefer to think of myself as spiritual. Anyway, I went through the process of being laicised –

made one of the people as opposed to one of the clergy – and Gloria and I got married. It was the best decision I ever made. No man ever wore a scarf as warm as Gloria's arms around my neck.'

'So, you're no longer a priest and you no longer have a parish.'

'I'm a former priest, that's true. But in another sense, I'm more of a priest than I've ever been. Look around you; this is my parish. These people are my flock. Whether they're Catholics or Protestants, believers or atheists, I care about them all. And over the last few years of working here, they have taken me to their hearts and when they have problems, they come to me and we chat, just like you and I are chatting.'

'But why here?'

'I felt drawn here. I started out as a trainer dealer, then became a dealer, then an inspector – managing a group of dealers – before being promoted to the position I'm in now, 'the pit boss', overseeing a whole section of the casino, mostly the poker hall.'

Father Jim paused.

'Today, I'm a broken, imperfect person exercising his ministry among broken, imperfect people and I wouldn't swap it for the world. I don't have facilities from a bishop to minister here but I do feel like I have a calling from God. I may not carry the title of a Father, but I carry the love of a father.'

Jake stared down at his pint glass, now less than half full.

'What's your story, Jake?'

'Well, seeing as you've been very honest with me, I will be honest with you.'

Jake pulled his hood down and for the next ten minutes narrated his story. He talked about his upbringing as a child in a fatherless family, with a depressed mother who denied him his freedom to create and explore. He talked of his undergraduate days and his teacher training, his first days at work and his climb up the ladder of promotion in a college of higher education. He spoke about meeting Sally, about her religious faith and her strong morals, her degree in psychology and her decision for a season to bring up children rather than go back to work. He described his two boys and paused to reflect – with a hint of pride and pleasure – about how different they were, even though they were both his. All this Jake narrated calmly, only occasionally allowing a flicker of emotion to pass across his face, before he at last plucked up the courage to speak about how he had left home.

Father Jim listened without interruption or censure as Jake's confession began. Jake told him about the events leading up to Christmas Eve, lowering his voice almost to a whisper as he did. He spoke about the slow descent into tedium at work and at home, his meeting with Pete and the thrill of poker playing. He moved on to the growing conflict and tension in his marriage and the sense of being restricted – no, trapped – by his wife. He explained that he had wanted to provide for his family and that this had been his motivation, at least at the beginning. He also shared about his longing to live while he still had life – adding, 'Life is not a dress rehearsal.'

Just as he said, that the barman picked up a hand bell and rang it three times, shouting 'Happy Christmas' and informing everyone that the bar was no longer open.

Father Jim stretched out his hand to shake Jake's as the two men stood to leave. 'If you ever need a listening ear or a helping hand, then I'm always here,' he said to Jake. 'Don't ever think I'm going to judge you. What with my story, I can't exactly take the moral high ground now, can I?'

They wished each other well, Father Jim adding, 'Good luck and Godspeed,' before Jake took his box of cash and wrapped it within the folds of his raincoat.

'That's wise,' Father Jim said, 'although you'll be clean foundered in this weather without your coat.'

'Is it dangerous outside?'

Father Jim nodded and replied. 'Aye, it can be. Although the police patrol the neighbourhood, it has been known for people to win a fortune at the tables and then lose it all on the streets in a savage beating. So, take care how you go. If you need a taxi, you can phone for one.'

'Oh no, I don't need one. I'm in walking distance.'

'Aye, okay,' Father Jim replied. 'You'll have to excuse me. Some of our friends over there have had a wee bit too much to drink and are fluthered. I'm going to shepherd them out of here.'

As he walked away towards a group of rowdy young men in the corner of the bar, Father Jim turned to Jake.

'Cheerio, my friend, it's been good to talk. And I hope you liked the Guinness!'

Jake nodded and walked towards the revolving doors at the front entrance of the casino, passing a group of Chinese husbands who were explaining to their wives just how much money they had won or lost at the roulette tables.

As Jake wandered out of the front doors he was met by an onslaught of freezing air which forced him to turn around and go back indoors, seeking shelter. He emptied the box he had been hiding and thrust the bricks of banknotes into every available pocket, before pulling his hood over his head and exiting the building once again.

Many of the customers had now left and it was mostly casino employees loitering outside, stamping down the hardening snow. As the falling snowflakes freckled their faces, some cupped their hands and blew hot breath into their fingers while wishing each other a 'very merry Christmas.' Others smoked cigarettes, marching on the spot to keep their feet warm, and sending billowing clouds of smoke into the night sky.

As Jake began to make his way down the road towards his hotel, he noticed out of the corner of his eye a tall, lean figure approaching him out of the darkness. As soon as he heard high-heeled shoes crunching into snow and tarmac, he knew it was Sandra. She had folded her hands underneath a thick shawl covered in bright white feathers. Her chin was tucked into the plumage and her eyes were peering over its edge at Jake.

'Mind if I walk with you?' she asked, steering her right hand into the narrow gap between Jake's left arm and his overcoat.

'Not at all,' Jake replied. 'It's not safe for a pretty young woman like you to be walking out this late alone.'

'I know,' Sandra replied, 'but I have to do it all the time, so I'm kind of used to it now.'

'Where's home?' Jake asked. 'I'm happy to get a taxi if it's any distance from here. I can walk you to your front door.'

Sandra laughed.

'Tell you what, why don't I escort you? I haven't seen you here before and if you're new to the area, you'll need someone to protect you.'

As soon as she said this, Sandra withdrew her arms from Jake's and swivelled 360 degrees, throwing her arms out sideways, and pulling her feathered shawl to its full length.

'See?' she said, giggling. 'I'm your guardian angel.'

Jake laughed. 'Sure thing. You can escort me. My hotel's just down the road. But then I'm getting a taxi for you.'

'We'll see about that,' Sandra replied, entwining her arm in his once again.

Jake and Sandra walked the rest of the way without talking. In their hearts, they both understood the choice that lay ahead of them. By the time the two of them approached the entrance of Jake's hotel, both had made it.

'Do you mind if I come in?' Sandra asked. 'It's Christmas. I'm alone. You seem like a nice guy. You looked after me in the casino tonight. You were polite, generous too. I really wouldn't mind the company, tonight of all nights.'

For one second, it seemed as if Sally's face appeared before Jake's eyes, looking into his with a confused and wounded gaze. Jake brushed it away like snow from his sleeve.

'Of course you can,' he said.

Sandra squealed into her white feathers and squeezed Jake's arm as the two of them entered the foyer of the hotel before slipping into the first lift door to open. As they ascended to the fourth floor, Sandra leant her head upon Jake's shoulder and yawned, releasing a short, high-pitched sigh like a puppy.

Jake stared at her in one of the mirrors inside the elevator. Sandra did not seem like someone who had manipulated her way into a conquest. She looked almost like a child, burying her pretty face and her lonely eyes into his chest, pulling the lapel of his coat over her head as if to shelter herself from the light. Within seconds, the two of them were at his door and then inside his room.

'Have a seat,' Jake said, pointing to an armchair next to the big blinds, which were still drawn. But Sandra had no intention of sitting down. As Jake turned to take off his hoodie, she stepped forward. 'Let me help you off with that,' she said, manoeuvring Jake's sweatshirt from his shoulders, after first taking down his hood. As she started to unbutton the top of his grandad T-shirt she moved closer, pressing her firm body into his, moving her lips towards his. As she moved down to the third button, their lips met.

Jake pulled away. 'I'm really sorry, Sandra,' he said. 'It's not you, I promise. It's just that I've only just left my wife and even though we are now separated, it just doesn't feel right.'

Sandra stepped back. 'That's okay. Do you want me to go?'

'No, I don't,' he said. 'I'd like you to stay but if I can be blunt, I just want your company, not your body.'

Sandra gasped. 'That's the first time a man has ever said that to me. Perhaps I will take a seat after all. And perhaps now would be a good time for you to tell me your name as well.'

Sandra removed her feathered shawl and sank into the armchair while Jake introduced himself, and then he rang room service to order a bottle of champagne and some smoked salmon sandwiches, which he paid for from the cash he had now locked inside the safe in his room. The two of them talked together long into the night, he lying on the bed with his head propped up on the pillows, she sitting in the chair, nursing and sipping her glass of champagne. They exchanged stories and made frivolous toasts, laughing loudly and drinking eagerly.

Jake was just reflecting that he could not remember ever having laughed so much with a woman when he felt a wave of tiredness breaking over his body.

'Don't think I'm rude,' he said. 'You are scintillating company, but I'm drifting off. I think it may be time for bed.'

Jake looked at his watch. 5 a.m.

'It's nearly daybreak!'

Sandra smiled, bared her bright white teeth, and said in a mock Transylvanian accent, 'You and I are creatures of the night.'

'We truly are,' Jake chortled as he sprung to his feet to go to the bathroom.

'Maybe we should have a couple of coffins set up in the casino basement,' Sandra joked. 'One for you and one for me.'

Jake chuckled as he entered the bathroom. When he came out a few minutes later, Sandra walked past him towards the basin. 'Mind if I use your toothbrush and toothpaste?' she shouted from within. 'I'm a very clean girl, I promise!'

'Be my guest,' Jake replied.

Jake had no night clothes with him, so he climbed into the large double bed wearing only his boxer shorts. He switched off all the lights and moved over to the left side of the bed, the opposite side to the one he'd occupied for so many years with Sally. The door to the bathroom opened and Sandra stood bathed in the light from inside. She was wearing a full-length white bathrobe. As Jake peered from the shadows, he guessed that she was not wearing much, if anything, underneath.

Sandra switched off the bathroom light and walked cautiously in the darkness to the right side of the bed. She reached out her hands and turned back the covers. Jake heard her bathrobe falling into a heap on the floor before the mattress began to move ever so slightly as she manoeuvred herself into the bed.

Lying with her back to Jake, Sandra whispered to him. 'Jake, I know you said you didn't want me right now, and I'm okay with that. But please could you just hold me? I really need a hug. I'm not after anything else. I just want your arms round me as I go to sleep.'

'Sure,' Jake said.

With that, he turned and reached out towards her. His hands touched her shoulders and as they did, she pulled his hands so that they were on top of hers, just above her stomach. Jake's chest brushed her back and their skin touched. He could not believe how soft and firm she seemed.

Jake drew closer to Sandra, who wriggled towards him, emitting a barely audible murmur of delight before falling fast asleep.

Jake smiled and thought, *I can still make a woman happy after all.*

Ten hours later, Jake woke disoriented. He didn't know where he was or who it was that was locked like a limpet onto his warm back. He stretched out his hand to the bedside table and looked at his watch. It was 4 p.m.

For a moment, Jake thought of phoning his boys and wishing them a happy Christmas, but then the guilt of sleeping with someone who was not their mother overwhelmed him, and he dismissed the thought outright.

Placing his watch back under the lamp, Jake turned to see Sandra lying beside him. The bedsheet and duvet were beneath her waist. For a moment, he gazed at her body and marvelled at its alluring symmetry. He had never seen such a perfectly proportioned figure in his entire life. *What was it that Father Jim called her?* he thought. Oh yes, *'a fine looking woman'.*

Jake took one more look before moving the bedsheets over Sandra's chest and walking to the bathroom. Later, as he opened the packet of one of the new shirts he had bought, the raw crack of the plastic startled Sandra. She woke and sat up, with the bedsheet lifted like a napkin under her chin. She looked at Jake. In fact, she studied him.

'You are gorgeous, Jake,' she said. 'You're really hot – so hot I'm going to need oven gloves next time I touch you.'

Jake laughed. 'No one has said anything like that to me in a very long time.'

Sandra grabbed the sheet and pulled it off the bed. Draping it toga-like over her body, she walked towards Jake on her way to the bathroom. She paused where Jake was standing, leant over and kissed him on the cheek.

'Happy Christmas, Jake. May all your dreams come true.'

'The same to you, Sandra,' he said, kissing her back.

For the next thirty minutes Jake, now dressed, sat on the bed and surfed the TV channels. He flitted from Christmas movie to Christmas movie – some in colour, others in black and white – until he found a sports channel showing the final table from the previous year's World Series of Poker in Vegas.

He studied hands and their players, enjoying the witty banter of the commentators but in truth enjoying more the intermittent squealing and exuberant splashing coming from the frothy bath where Sandra was wallowing. Half an hour later, Sandra was dressed and putting on her make-up in front of a mirror in the bedroom.

'The casino is closed on Christmas Day,' she said. 'It opens again at midnight. What do you want to do until then?'

'I'm really hungry. Let's see if the hotel can cook up Christmas dinner for us.'

'You are the cutest!' Sandra said.

Jake and Sandra left the room and made their way to reception. They walked to the bar for a cocktail before being seated at a restaurant table by Tom, the hotel manager, who brought two green and red crackers.

'These are on the house.'

Jake and Sandra pulled their crackers and put on paper hats before embarking on a full Christmas dinner, accompanied by the sound of Christmas carols playing in the restaurant.

'I have always loved this one,' Sandra said as she quietly sang, 'While mortals sleep, the angels keep their watch of wondering love.'

For a while, they both kept silent. When the carol ended, Jake and Sandra returned to their food and to their conversation. An hour later, Jake paid the bill in cash and Sandra thanked him.

'Are you going to come with me to the casino tonight?' she asked.

'Of course. I'm going to try the cash tables this time.'

'Great,' Sandra replied. 'Let's walk over there together.'

Two hours later Sandra and Jake were walking arm in arm through the snow, steadying each other on the ice.

That night Sandra served at the tables while the Monk, suitably attired with his grey hood, played at the poker tables. She kept a special eye on Jake, touching him from time to time, just to let him know she was there. At no point did Jake need to break his concentration and turn around to see who it was. He knew from the way she rested her hand upon his shoulder that it was her.

Throughout the night Jake played with an intensity he had never known before, conquering three out of the four tables that he played, adding over £1,000 to the cash he'd brought.

After the sun had risen, he and Sandra returned to the hotel to have a full English breakfast in their room before falling asleep exhausted in each other's arms.

The next evening, the Monk played again.

And he prospered again.

Two days later, Jake paid Tom in cash for his room for the week. Four days after that, Jake and Sandra kissed on New Year's Eve and later that night went from being friends to being lovers.

———

Over the subsequent months, the Monk's reputation as a poker player grew and his relationship with Sandra deepened.

Jake won five out of eight tournaments he entered and averaged £1,000 winnings a night at the cash tables. He never donned designer shirts and suits, preferring to keep to his grey hoodie. He did, however, replace his silver saloon with a black Porsche and bought new clothes and jewellery for Sandra, and he flew with her to exotic European cities to play against the foreign stars.

When summer gave way to autumn, Jake moved into the Penthouse Suite on the top floor of his hotel: a spacious set of rooms with a large and luxurious lounge, whose greatest asset was a 60-inch HD television connected to a discrete, state-of-the-art surround sound system, which hung like a techno masterpiece above a white marble fireplace.

The Monk had now made a name for himself in the casino. He became the player to beat, and every emerging and experienced talent in the region made it their goal to take his money, but none could match his uncanny ability to read opponents or his skill at assessing probabilities. Jake was quite simply at the top of his game and no one, it seemed, could compete with him.

Except, that is, one. The Undertaker, as he was known, was a skinny man who dressed in a top hat and tails like a Victorian pall bearer. He had skeletal fingers with long unkempt nails which he used to scratch his Pocket Cards before revealing them. His teeth were stained yellow from smoking – a habit that had left him with a rattle when he inhaled. He was rarely seen or heard in the casinos these days; his favoured venues were the private homes of local men and women who had made their fortunes through crime or business, or a mixture of the two. There he would play cash games, with buy-ins far bigger than any casino and prizes greater than anything ever won there either.

No one had ever conquered the Undertaker in the private homes where vast amounts of money were gambled between the hours of midnight and daybreak. Many wealthy businessmen and women had tried to beat him but had ended up losing face and fortune. Experienced gamblers had tried and failed. Even hardened gangsters had pitted their wits against him but had come away with a beating, vowing – sometimes shaking their blood-drained faces – never to play him again.

One autumn night, the Monk felt an unfamiliar touch upon his shoulder in his local casino where he had just won £2,000 at a cash table, fleecing eight cocky twenty-year-olds of their money. It was 3 a.m. and Jake was ready to go to the casino restaurant for an espresso. He knew straight away that it wasn't Sandra. This hand was cold, sending a reverberating chill into his upper torso, and the fingernails dug into his shoulder, causing him to shudder before turning. When he looked round, he saw a man in black, dressed from head-to-toe like a funeral director. *Death.*

Jake stood up, overshadowed by the man, who was over six feet four inches tall. The Undertaker handed Jake a gilded white card. It was an invitation to play a game of poker that night at a private mansion half an hour away. The card informed him that a limousine was waiting which would take him there and bring him back. The buy-in was £1,000 and the game was No Limit Texas Hold'em.

Jake looked up from the invitation to see that the Undertaker had already taken several steps away, and had turned to look back at Jake with eyes that were squinting under the blazing bulbs of a lowering chandelier.

Jake paused, looked at the invitation, then turned his attention back to the macabre messenger. The Undertaker's left arm was stretched out towards him, his bony hand emerging out of his black coat, his sharp and sinewy index finger beckoning him to follow.

Jake knew with a primal intuition this man was dangerous, but he had already made his choice. Just a few days earlier, he had decided that his days of cautious gambling were over. Up until then he had played with a view to make enough money to enjoy an extravagant lifestyle. Now that he had achieved that, he was becoming bored. He remembered something Pete had said to him, that most successful poker players get to a point where they know they can only win big if they risk big.

As the Undertaker turned to leave, Jake followed in his wake, keeping just a few steps behind him, watching as the staff and players in the casino moved aside to let the shadowy figure pass.

As the Monk left the casino through the revolving doors, he felt a sudden jolt of responsibility and cast a glance behind him to see if Sandra was there. *She'll have to walk back to the hotel herself tonight, Jake thought.*

Outside, the Undertaker was standing beside a long, black limousine. A man in a suit and cap, with shoulders that made him look as wide as he was long, stepped out of the driver's side of the car and walked to the back door and opened it. Jake entered and sat on one of the forward-facing leather seats.

The Undertaker sat opposite him and said nothing. A moment later, the car was gliding smoothly on the icy road from the casino out into the city, whose streets were populated only by a smattering of girls in tight, short skirts.

'Where are we going?' Jake asked as the sleek vehicle slid underneath the illuminated wings of the Angel of the North.

The Undertaker put the bony index finger of his left hand to his lips to indicate that the location was a secret.

Jake looked away and stared out the window of the car as it sped through the night. He saw the shapes of looming trees and hedgerows until he became aware that the vehicle had turned off a main road and was making its way on a drive through some fields. After about a minute, the limo slowed down and paused before some cast iron gates. The chauffeur spoke into an intercom and the gates moved inwards until the path was clear.

Jake leaned forward to peer past the Undertaker through the front windows of the car. They were on a road leading up a slight incline to a mansion illuminated by Victorian street lights. The three-storey building was the size of a small country house, with strong white pillars around the porch and an enormous mullioned window above it, a chandelier pulsating with warm light from inside.

As the car came to a halt, the chauffeur opened the door and the Undertaker and his guest strode towards the large oak door. The next moment, a man in a black suit let them in and the two men marched through a panelled foyer, down a darkened corridor to a room whose half-opened door was leaking light and smoke.

As Jake followed his silent guide, he found himself in a library bigger than his entire house. There were leather bound books on every shelf, with mobile stepladders for volumes out of reach. In the centre of the room there was a poker table, with eight men seated at it. Most had enormous wine or brandy glasses next to them on brass trolleys. Several had Cuban cigars in their hands or mouths, filling the entire room with an almost overwhelming smell of heavy tobacco.

'Behold the Monk!' a voice bellowed.

Jake peered into the smoke and saw a short, rotund man with greased-back black hair and a blood-red smoking jacket beckoning him to the table. *Control*.

'We've been hearing a great deal about you,' he continued, moving both his hands outwards to include the men around the table – most of whom did not acknowledge Jake's presence.

'Come and sit down,' he said.

The man in the red jacket sat down himself while a young, blonde woman took Jake's arm and led him to an unoccupied seat. She was dressed in a sparkling pearl-coloured dress which left little to Jake's imagination. All her movements were exaggerated, designed to emphasise the curves of her body. As the two of them reached the table, the girl smiled seductively before drawing a gold-painted chair so that Jake could sit.

'Play,' the man with the smoking jacket boomed.

Jake paused and took stock, looking round the table. He had never seen such a diverse group of players before. To his left there was a man who was from an Arab background. To his right there was a man who looked like a Russian, and talked like one as well. The men either side of him were oriental. The rest were Irish, South American and Indian. All of them were decked with emblems of opulence and power. Jake smelled money – lots of it.

The only other person within Jake's field of vision was the Undertaker. He was not sitting at the table but stood behind the host with his hands by his side, as if on sentry duty.

The Monk took a deep breath. He put his hand inside his pocket and removed a brick of banknotes. For the first time, the other players began to look at Jake, their eyes widening as they saw the money.

Jake counted out £1,000 in a deliberate and unhurried way before tossing it almost carelessly into the centre of the table.

He then placed the remaining notes inside his pocket before raising his head and his voice.

'Shuffle up and deal,' he said.

Out of the gloom a buxom woman moved to the table, took a pack of brand-new playing cards, and spread them in a perfect crescent shape across the bright red surface of the table. She shuffled them before dealing out the Pocket Cards to every player.

Jake, being in the big blind, waited his turn. The player right behind him was the Russian. No one had bet by the time his turn came. When he picked up his two cards Jake spotted a tell-tale read from the Russian – the black pupils of his eyes constricted a matter of a tenth of an inch.

'Call and raise to £200,' the Russian said.

Jake knew what was happening. In his mind, it was a well-telegraphed attempt to bluff Jake and get him to give up the £100 he'd put in for the big blind. Jake, sensing this early – if not premature – power play, looked at the corner of his cards. He had a Pair of Queens. He called the Russian and raised £200. All the players who had put in money to see the flop folded. This just left Jake and the Russian.

Jake noticed a bead of sweat on the man's brow, just above his thick black eyebrows. The Russian was about to commit his entire stack.

'All-in,' he said, pushing the remainder of his notes into the middle of the table.

'I call,' Jake said, revealing his two Queens.

The Russian growled like a wounded wolf and stood bolt upright.

'I've had enough,' he snarled, before snatching a black leather jacket from the back of his chair and storming off with a fat, unlit cigar he had snatched from a gilded box on the table.

There was a gasp.

Jake watched as the two oriental players leaned towards each other and whispered something. And he noted a brief exchange between his host and the Undertaker, who had bowed low to hear some instructions. The Undertaker nodded and then left before the host informed the table that it was time to start again.

'Deal!' he roared.

Jake took down one player after another, beginning with the Irishman – a likeable rogue with a tendency to talk too much, and reveal too much as well. The last man standing, besides Jake, was the host. In a heads-up battle that lasted ten minutes, Jake defeated him as well, winning a final stack of over £10,000.

Jake licked his lips and swept the money into his arms, arranging the notes into piles of £10, £20 and £50. The blonde woman in the pearl-white dress returned with a black briefcase, into which he placed his banknotes. He gave her a £20 note and left two £50 notes for the dealer.

Jake looked at his watch. It was 8 a.m. He had been playing for nearly five hours. When he looked up again, the Undertaker was standing right in front of him, beckoning him to walk with him to the heavy oak door at the front of the house. He pointed to the limo outside and Jake walked towards its open door, flanked by the suited chauffeur. As the sleek vehicle pulled away down the drive, Jake noticed that the host and the Undertaker were talking to each other again in front of the house.

Half an hour later, Jake was in his hotel lobby, rubbing his eyes that were still stinging from the cigar smoke. He entered the lift and arrived at the top floor. 'Sandra,' he said to himself as he arrived at his Penthouse Suite.

He snuck on tiptoe through the sitting room, already enjoying the thought of snuggling up to his girl. He removed his shoes and entered the bedroom. The big blinds were drawn as they always were and Jake could still make out the posts and drapes of the bed they shared. But as he stepped to the side of the bed he could see that it was empty. The bed had not been slept in. *She should have been back hours ago,* Jake thought.

A phone call to reception revealed that Sandra had not returned and there were no messages from her either. A further call to Father Jim at the casino confirmed that she had left work at the normal time – 7 a.m. She had not, however, completed the short journey from the casino to the hotel.

Jake sat down on the side of the bed and tried to work out what Sandra might have done. It was too early for her to have gone shopping and she never went anywhere else for breakfast. They always shared a healthy meal brought by room service to the dining room in their suite on returning from the casino. There was nowhere else, Jake figured, she could have gone. She had moved out of her bedsit to live with him months ago. And in any case, Sandra would have texted him if she had decided to go off for coffee with one of her work friends.

As morning turned to noon, Jake sat in an armchair in the sitting room, waiting for Sandra to return. From time to time he nodded off, only waking when his hooded head dropped upon his chest. As the day lengthened, Jake's anxiety deepened. When it was Sandra's time to start work, he ran up to the casino, pushed through the revolving doors and dashed into the foyer, his eyes darting from one woman to another. It was only when Father Jim informed him that she had not come into work, nor had she left a message with her line manager, that his anxiety began to morph into fear.

'What can have happened to her?' Jake asked.

'I don't know, Jake. Let's phone the police.'

Fifteen minutes later two uniformed officers were standing in the bar area, asking Jake for a full description of Sandra. As Jake talked about her, tears began to form in his eyes. Father Jim took over and the two officers filled in a missing person's report and then left.

Jake spent all night at the casino, sitting in the downstairs bar at a table affording a good view of the entrance. Hour after hour until dawn he kept his vigil, hoping that Sandra would come running into the foyer, her white feather shawl around her neck, her eager eyes looking and longing for his.

As the night staff gave way to their replacements, Jake sighed and got to his feet. Father Jim, who had sat with him from time to time throughout the night, appeared by his side.

'Jake, you can't help Sandra if you're exhausted. Go back to your hotel and get some sleep. I have your mobile number and the hotel number, too. I'll stay on here today and look out for her. I'll phone you if I hear of anything.'

Jake nodded and wandered wearily from the casino down the road to his hotel. Within minutes he was in his king-size bed, sleeping restlessly. From time to time he turned over and reached out for Sandra, thinking she was there – as she had been each night for many months – but every time his desperate hands met empty space. And every time a wave of disappointment broke upon him.

Eight hours into his sleep, the telephone chimed. It was Tom in reception.

'There are two police officers here to see you. Shall I bring them up?'

Jake felt the blood drain from his face.

'Yes.'

Two minutes later, the three men arrived.

'You'd better sit down, sir,' one of them said.

'No, I'm alright.'

The second police officer took over. 'I'm sorry to say we've found the body of a young woman half a mile from the Angel. It answers the description you've given us of Sandra. Could you come to the station?'

Jake felt dizzy.

Half an hour later, the same police officer drew a white sheet back to reveal Sandra's pale face, beautiful and lonely in death.

'It's her,' he stuttered.

'I'm sorry, sir.'

'Who could have done such a thing?'

'Whoever it was drove her to the Angel sometime between the hours of four and six in the morning. They used her shawl to strangle her. We found it lying next to her. There were white feathers everywhere.'

Jake's head began to spin.

The officer brought a chair to Sandra's side and Jake sat, pulling aside the white sheet and taking Sandra's bleached, soft hand in his. He squeezed it, hoping she would squeal and say, 'Jake, you're the cutest.'

At that moment Father Jim came through the door, escorted by a uniformed, female police officer. The two officers left the chilly room, leaving Father Jim the other side of the bed from Jake. He didn't say a word to Jake. He held Sandra's other hand in his. He bowed his head and closed his sad eyes and began to pray. Jake was only conscious of a few phrases. Unfamiliar though the words were, and the faith from which they had been forged, he knew in his heart they were needed.

'Show mercy upon the soul of thy servant Sandra... Place her in the region of peace and light... eternal rest give unto her and let perpetual light shine upon her.'

And as Father Jim concluded with the words, 'may she rest in peace,' Jake found himself saying, 'Amen.'

It was several weeks later that Sandra's funeral took place. There had to be an autopsy and then some further investigations before the body was released for burial.

A service was held behind closed doors for family only, which turned out to be Sandra's father and mother. None of Sandra's casino family was invited. Instead, a group of her female colleagues had gone to Father Jim and asked him to say some prayers at the poker tables where she served. They didn't want a priest or vicar pontificating over someone he had never met, in a church they had never attended. They wanted him – Father Jim.

On the same day and time as the funeral, Jake walked into the casino wearing his best suit and overcoat. Everyone – both employees and players – were asked to stop what they were doing and observe two minutes of silence as a mark of respect. Upstairs in the poker room, scores of people stood and bowed. Father Jim stood at the centre with a microphone in his hand, and Jake by his side. Many of the female staff wept.

Father Jim encouraged everyone to think of just one thing they loved about Sandra and hold it in their hearts. For Jake, a hundred memories came, but one stood above them all. Sandra had always loved to wear her feather shawl and had joked that she was endowed with angel's wings. Right from the beginning of their relationship, Sandra had always somehow known when Jake was thinking of home. She had never asked why. Instead she had gone to her shawl, plucked a white feather and placed it in his hands, as a sign to him that she understood.

As Jake smiled, Father Jim began to pray. 'God our Father, your power brings us to birth; your providence guides our lives, and by your command we return to dust. Lord, those who die still live in your presence; their lives change but do not end. We pray in hope for our loved one Sandra. In company with the Lord Jesus, who died and now lives, may she rejoice in your kingdom where all our tears are wiped away; unite us together in one family, to sing your praise forever and ever, Amen.'

Everyone in the casino said, 'Amen.'

Father Jim turned his face to look at those who were standing for Sandra. 'Thank you for showing Sandra such respect. I know she'd appreciate how many have turned out. Whether you are a player or a worker here, keep her memory alive in your hearts. Pray that the police will discover Sandra's murderer and that he will be brought to justice. Pray for her family to be comforted and for those who loved her most find peace. That's all. Good luck and Godspeed.'

As Father Jim concluded, several of Sandra's friends began to clap. It was only two or three at first, but then more began to pick it up. Soon every single person was applauding, some for the way that Father Jim had said his piece, but mostly because they wanted to celebrate their friend.

When Jake finished clapping too, he turned to leave the poker room and as he did he put his hands in the outer pockets of his coat. As soon as he did he was aware of something soft touching his fingers.

'What the...?'

Drawing his hands up to his face, he stared as white feathers began to fall through his fingers, spiralling down to the carpet.

He gasped and fell to his knees.

Father Jim drew near to Jake and put his hand on his shoulder. 'What's this?' he asked.

'I don't know. I just reached inside my pockets and there they were... white feathers, like the ones Sandra used to wear around her shoulders.'

Father Jim squeezed Jake's shoulder and then walked off.

As Jake left the building, there was a subdued atmosphere throughout the casino. Gaming terminals were still playing their jingles, but it seemed to Jake as if the normal hubbub had been put on mute.

Jake walked down the slope from the casino to his hotel and lay on a sofa in his sitting room. He slept intermittently, waking from dreams of Sandra calling to him from the cold.

That night he washed and walked again to the casino. He hadn't shaved in several days and the stubble was beginning to show, as were the bags beneath his tear-stretched eyes. For the first time since he had taken up poker he played without feeling, his hands and brain moving in mechanistic unison at the table.

For the next few weeks he won more and more, but cared less and less. Needing company, he contacted a local escort agency and was seen with two young women, one on either arm, both with low-cut dresses and fake diamond necklaces.

One night, when Jake was taking a break and the two girls had gone to powder their noses, Father Jim sidled up to the bar where Jake had roosted.

'How are you, Jake?'

'I'm coping.'

'So it seems, from the company you're keeping.'

'They're not Sandra.'

'No, they're not.' Father Jim paused before adding, 'One word of advice. Beware the painted ladies.'

As the two women returned, Jake stood with the two cocktails he had ordered. They took the glasses with their sticks and fruit and parasols before fastening themselves onto their provider's arms and accompanying him with a swagger to the poker table. There they stood just behind him, their eyes expanding and sparkling every time he won a hand and pulled a stash of notes into his lap.

At dawn, they left through the revolving doors and returned with Jake to his rooms where a continental breakfast – with champagne and strawberries – was followed by a hot tub together and then sleep.

Late in the afternoon Jake awoke to find the girls had gone. Looking at his reflection in the bathroom mirror, he observed bright red marks on his face, neck and chest, like lurid smudges on an artist's pallet. It was a few minutes before he realised what it was: faded lipstick from the painted ladies. Jake scrubbed the stains off in the shower before going to the buffet at the hotel restaurant. Then it was off to the casino to begin the same routine, this time with two different girls.

After a month of this, Jake had already become bored.

One night in the casino, he baulked at the thought of escort girls with tight dresses and bright lips and broke away from all the preening players lining up at his table to take a shot at beating him.

Jake made his way to the bar and made it clear to all the poker puppies yapping at his heels that he wanted to be left alone. He sat at a table staring into the 'black stuff' and looking on his phone at photos of Sandra in her feather shawl.

Half an hour of this and his frozen heart began to thaw. Tears filled his eyes as he thought of his angel. Grief assaulted the castle of his heart, and with it came a sudden charge of guilt that bridged the moat and breached the walls he had built.

If I had walked her back as I always had, he thought, *she would still be alive.*

As soon as Jake uttered these silent words, a further pang of guilt struck his heart. He put his head in his hands. Jake began to groan as he wiped his eyes and as he did, he saw Father Jim.

Father Jim placed his hand upon Jake's arm.

'This is not your fault.'

'I should have been there.'

Father Jim leaned forward. 'Do you think Sandra would want you to feel guilty?'

'Sandra can't feel anything.'

'But if her soul was still alive, do you think she would be happy to see you in such turmoil? I don't think so. And do you think she would be pleased to see you trying to find comfort in the arms of women who are even more tormented than you are?'

'They don't comfort me.'

'But Sandra did, didn't she?'

'Yes.'

'When you were in her arms, the guilt left you, didn't it?'

'What guilt?'

'The one you never talk about, the one that wakes you up when you're asleep.'

Jake grimaced.

'Even monks need to confess sometimes,' Jim said.

Jake could not speak.

Father Jim lifted his hand from Jake's arm to his shoulder and rested it there. Then he leaned over and whispered, 'One thing I can say, one thing I've learned from decades as a priest, is that the greatest gift of all is the ability to give and to receive forgiveness. And sometimes the person you most need to forgive is yourself.'

With that, Father Jim walked away.

Jake dragged himself to his feet and sloped back to his hotel, where he drank a small bottle of whiskey before falling into his half-empty bed.

The following night, the snow began to fall again. It was just before Christmas. Jake was milling in the bar at the end of a lucrative night playing at the tables when he felt a tap on his shoulder. He turned, for a moment hoping it was Sandra, only to see the towering figure of the Undertaker. Jake had not seen nor heard of the man's whereabouts since the night Sandra died. He had often wondered, in the tedium of his easy conquests in the casino, if the Undertaker was watching from some hidden vantage point, like a weather-beaten crow perched on some high and invisible branch. He had also hoped that the Undertaker would appear in the casino again to take him back to private games in exotic mansions where serious players and real money were to be found. Now the Undertaker was back, with a face as grey and lifeless as a gravestone.

The interloper said nothing, but simply handed him a white invitation card, gilded with gold, just as he had before. Jake took it and read:

HEADS-UP COMPETITION. BUY-IN £100,000. RE-BUY UP TO £150,000. TOURNAMENT OF THE YEAR. CHRISTMAS EVE. BY INVITATION ONLY.

'Who are the two players?' he asked.

The Undertaker reached out his hand and placed a finger on Jake's heart before reaching back to point at his own.

'You and me?' Jake asked.

The Undertaker nodded.

For a moment Jake paused and considered the odds. *£250,000 is more than I have*, he thought, *but I've got to risk big if I'm going to win big.*

Jake looked at the Undertaker. 'Where is this taking place?'

The Undertaker turned the card over and showed Jake the address. An apartment overlooking the river, about two miles from the casino.

Jake felt a sudden rush as he imagined the super-rich from far and near gathering around a poker table, watching him take the Undertaker down in a make-or-break duel at dawn.

'I'll be there – eight o'clock in the evening, the night before Christmas,' he said.

The Undertaker drew his index finger out again and scratched the bottom of the card with his nail.

DRESS CODE FORMAL. SUITS AND TIES ONLY.

Jake paused. He had built his alternative poker identity around his grey hoodie. Admittedly it was darker than it had been, faded by constant use, and frayed at the edges. But it was his house sigil, his battle standard, his defence against the night. The prize, however, persuaded him.

Jake placed the invitation card in his pocket and reached out his right hand to the Undertaker. 'Very well. May the best man win.'

But the Undertaker did not reply, nor did he take Jake's hand. He turned to leave, and as he did so, stopped in his tracks. Unknown to him – and indeed to Jake – Father Jim had appeared while the two men were in the bar. When he turned, the Undertaker was caught off-guard. For once his face cracked like an old mirror, turning from shock before becoming transfixed in contempt.

'You are not welcome here,' Father Jim said calmly. 'Leave now.'

The Undertaker said nothing, but made as if to brush the former priest aside. But Father Jim was not going anywhere. He stood his ground.

The Undertaker breathed loudly, his throat rasping as he did. He stepped to his right and walked briskly out of the casino.

As Jake looked on, Father Jim stepped right in front of him.

'Careful now, my friend,' he said. 'The beast has outwitted many a monk.'

'I know what I'm doing,' Jake said.

Jake had calculated that he had £205,000 in cash from twelve months of winnings, all kept under lock and key in the hotel safe. He also realised that he needed to win another £45,000 and quickly.

Over the next five nights Jake spent two four-hour stints at the cash tables, winning a further £15,000 with some electric displays of aggressive poker. But he was still £30,000 short of the total needed buy in again if he found himself down in his heads-up match with the Undertaker. He would just have to make sure he stayed on top.

On Christmas Eve at 7.30 p.m., Jake Graystone dressed in a black suit, white shirt, black tie and gleaming, brand-new shoes. He donned his overcoat and picked up a security case with a special combination and filled it with £220,000 in cash. He bade Tom a happy Christmas and walked to his Porsche in the hotel car park. He set his satnav system to the coordinates on the ornate invitation card and relished the throaty roar of the engine. In no time at all, he was standing outside a brand-new sixty floor building made entirely, it seemed, of darkened glass, with tiny flakes of snow disappearing into every pane.

The same woman Jake had seen at the private mansion appeared, clothed in a long, blood-red ball gown and a thick fur shawl. Within fifteen minutes he had shaken hands with his host, handed over his cash and was seated at one end of a full-sized poker table. A dealer was standing in the centre of the table facing four rows of chairs accommodating thirty spectators, who were chatting with anticipation and chinking their champagne glasses as they agreed how much they were going to wager and on whom.

A grandfather clock sounded eight chimes. The Undertaker appeared from a room behind the table. The rich spectators fell silent as the Undertaker sat the opposite end of the table in his top hat, staring past Jake through the tinted glass windows of the apartment at the night sky beyond.

The host greeted his visitors, explained they were welcome to use the bar during the breaks and that this heads-up tournament would last until one man had triumphed. He introduced Jake and the Undertaker, listing their triumphs and extolling their skills, as if he was the referee of a prize fight between champion boxers. He pointed to a large TV monitor clearly visible on the wall behind the dealer, and explained that it would show what the blinds were and provide a countdown to whenever the blinds increased. As the coup de grâce, he alerted his guests to some headphones underneath their chairs. These, he said, would provide an audio commentary on each round, with expert analysis provided by two former British poker champions whom he had hired for the evening – watching in an especially designed booth containing TV monitors.

'No expense has been spared,' he concluded, 'in the provision of a Christmas Eve to remember.'

As he finished, the room erupted with applause.

'Okay,' he added, 'shuffle up and deal.'

Each spectator placed their headsets over their ears.

During the initial skirmishes, it became clear to Jake that his adversary was of an altogether different class from anyone he had played. The Undertaker was a brilliant tactician, assessing probabilities with a brain that processed numbers and equations with the speed of a pocket calculator. Furthermore, his expressions were almost completely impassive, making it nigh-on impossible for Jake to get a read, even using his special gift.

Within two hours, Jake had lost £50,000. By midnight – the time assigned for a break – Jake had lost a further £50,000 and had to negotiate to buy in to the game again.

But Jake was £30,000 short if he was to need the full buy-in amount.

'What if I give you the keys to my Porsche?' Jake asked the host. 'It must be worth at least £30,000, even second-hand.'

'I'll not take more than £20,000 for it,' the host said, after a brief, whispered exchange with The Undertaker. 'You'll have to write an IOU for the rest.'

Jake agreed and then retired to a luxurious green room to reconsider his strategy.

In the first hand after the break, Jake went into super aggressive mode. He was dealt a Seven of Clubs and a Two of Hearts, the worst hand in poker, but he managed to bluff the Undertaker on the River, and win a large pot.

Over the course of the next two-and-a-half hours, the Undertaker took one hit after another until he had lost £100,000 and had to buy in again. He never said a word, even when he lost £50,000 more in one hand. In fact, he didn't say anything all night.

At three o'clock in the morning, the Undertaker had lost all the money he had won in the first half and the two stacks were pretty even. Jake had £220,000 and the Undertaker had £250,000.

For the next two hours, the players varied their game again, opting to play tight and carefree at the same time. By the time the first colours of dawn were beginning to dye the leaden skies outside, both players had barely moved from the place they had been two hours previously. It seemed like a stalemate.

At just past five o'clock, a final break was allowed. Jake went to a washroom and splashed cold water on his face. He stared into his bloodshot eyes and urged himself on for one final push. He drank a latte, with two extra shots, before sitting back down at the table as the clock chimed six times.

The Undertaker now retook his seat before the host reappeared and called the spectators to quieten down, adding that it was now time for the dealer to be replaced. As he said this, a slim young woman in a black dress appeared from the room from which the host and the Undertaker had just emerged. She had dark hair and brown eyes. And she was wearing a shawl made of white ostrich feathers.

As soon as Jake saw her, he gasped.

The woman looked like Sandra, only it wasn't her.

With that recognition, a hundred thoughts went running through his head. *Was this just a coincidence? Was this an intentional ploy to throw him off his game? If it was, had he known Sandra? If he had known her, did he kill her? Why did she have to die? What possible motive could there have been for the Undertaker killing her?*

Beads of sweat began to glisten on Jake's forehead and the faintest trace of a smile appeared at the same time in the corners of the Undertaker's mouth. Jake had been tilted.

There was no way now he could manage his emotions and remain rational and calm with a dealer like this.

Everything came to a head a few hands later when Jake was dealt a Pair of Queens as Pocket Cards. He knew that in a heads-up situation this was a good hand, but he also knew that in normal poker play this was one he always played with great care. This time, however, dazed by the Sandra lookalike in front of him, he cast caution to the winter wind.

Jake was in the small blind position and decided not only to call but also to raise the big blind (now £5,000), pushing chips worth £10,000 into the middle. The Undertaker paused for several moments before committing the same amount. The two players were now ready to see the flop.

The dealer placed one card face-down on the table before revealing three cards face-up – the King of Hearts, the King of Clubs, and the Queen of Diamonds. Jake had flopped a Full House – three Queens and two Kings.

Jake tried hard to disguise his elation. He didn't even bother to assess probabilities. As far as he was concerned, he had the winning hand.

I wish the real Sandra was here to see this, he thought.

The Undertaker studied Jake for a minute, squinting as he did so. With calculated precision, he counted out £25,000 chips and pushed them into the middle. Jake counted £25,000 in chips, and then a further £50,000.

'Raise you £50,000,' he said, as the chips began to tumble like toy buildings into one another.

The Undertaker gazed at Jake before counting out £50,000 and then a further £100,000. He pointed his index finger upwards to indicate to the dealer that he was raising the bet. The audience gasped as he pushed his chips into the centre.

Jake looked at the dealer again, wishing for a moment it was Sandra, longing for her calming presence. He was sure that the Undertaker was trying to bluff him, especially since his opponent had held off pushing all-in, leaving a small stack back as a safety net. But as he counted his chips, Jake realised he was short of £30,000 to call his adversary, never mind raise the bet.

The host approached the table.

'What do you propose?' he asked.

'The keys to my Porsche, please,' Jake said. 'And a paper and pen.'

The host looked at the Undertaker, who nodded in agreement.

The dealer leant forward and held out a piece of paper and a Montblanc pen. As she did, the feathers of her shawl touched Jake's hand. He shuddered and pulled his hand away, lifting it to his face in a wiping motion. As he did, the woman's fragrance filled his nostrils. It was the same perfume that Sandra had used.

Jake thought he was going to faint. The walls of the room seemed to slip out of their groves and start to move upwards and sideways, as if the laws of gravity had been suspended and he was in some unstable, parallel universe.

Get a grip! Jake thought.

He calmed his breathing and closed his eyes.

Then he took the pen, wrote out a note and signed it.

The dealer took the piece of paper and placed it in the middle of the table, on top of a small mountain of chips.

'Continue the game,' the host said.

Jake and the Undertaker rose to their feet. Every spectator did the same.

The dealer placed a card face-down and then revealed the fourth card – the Deuce of Clubs, irrelevant as far as Jake was concerned. She waited for a minute before placing another card face-down on the table, then revealing the fifth and final River Card – the Nine of Hearts.

Five cards were now face-up on the blood red cover of the poker table: The King of Hearts, King of Clubs, Queen of Diamonds, Deuce of Clubs, and the Nine of Hearts. Nothing had changed for Jake since the flop; he still had a Full House – three Queens and two Kings. As far as he was concerned, he was about to take the Undertaker down, leaving his opponent short stacked with about twenty grand in chips.

Jake placed his Pocket Cards on the table, face-up.

The small crowd clapped.

'Full House, Queens on Kings,' the host declared.

Now it was the Undertaker's turn. As Jake looked at him, it dawned on him that his opponent seemed unperturbed. Jake hadn't even considered the probability that the Undertaker had a better hand. In the wake of the appearance of the dealer, with her white feathered shawl, he had been in full tilt. Now it was the moment of truth, and Jake sensed to his horror that he might have been beaten.

The Undertaker revealed one of his two cards – the King of Hearts.

Jake went into a tail spin.

Father Jim's warning, '*Beware the painted ladies,*' flashed like a neon sign before his mind.

The spectators were now frenzied with anticipation.

'Hush now,' the host said, and the room fell silent. 'Please reveal your final card.'

The Undertaker took hold of the card, still face-down on the table. He turned it and placed it in the centre.

The King of Spades.

When Jake saw it, it was like a shotgun going off in his face. His Full House had been beaten by Quads – four Kings. His unbeatable hand had been beaten.

The audience clapped.

The host shook the Undertaker's hand.

Jake slumped into his seat.

The host took one of Jake's hands.

'Here, you'll need this,' he said, placing a piece of paper in his palm. 'These are the details of my bank account.'

Jake stared at the name of a bank that only wealthy people used, and the numbers of sort codes, accounts and dates.

'You must pay within twenty-four hours.'

'What if I can't?' Jake replied. 'It's Christmas Day. The casinos aren't open. I won't have a chance to win back ten grand that soon.'

'If you don't,' the host replied, 'you'll find out why your opponent is called the Undertaker.'

'You're kidding,' Jake exclaimed.

'No, I'm not. I'm deadly serious. With him, it's money or blood. Pay up or check out… permanently.'

The host pulled away, his appearance morphing from threat to charm as he shook the hands of the guests.

Jake took a few moments longer at the table, waiting for an opportunity to leave. He found it when the Undertaker became surrounded by members of the audience and the VIP guests.

Jake took one last look at the woman with the feather shawl before making his exit from the spacious lounge and lifting his overcoat from a hook beside the entrance to the flat. He strode from the apartment to the elevator and descended to the ground floor, where he walked in as normal a way as he could past the man on security and out the front entrance onto the street.

The snow had been falling all night and the pavements were covered with a thin white coating. Jake drew his lapels up to his neck. He went from walking fast to jogging and then from a jog to a full run. He had no idea where he was going. He couldn't return to his hotel. That would be the first place the Undertaker would look and, in any case, Jake had not yet paid his next bill. He considered running to the casino and asking Father Jim for help, but then remembered it was Christmas Day, the one day when the casino closed, and with that another door of hope slammed shut.

Jake thrust his freezing hands into the pockets of his overcoat as he continued to run. He wanted to return home, to the warmth of the fire in his living room, the Christmas tree, the presents, his boys, his ever so ordinary life, and Sally. But then a darker mood fell like a shadow upon his soul.

They won't want to see me, he thought. *I've caused them too much pain.*

He began to perspire as he sped through snow without direction.

And then the realisation began to take hold of him like a hangman's noose, asphyxiating all hope from his fractured mind.

I'm homeless.

Dear daddy

Mummy says I'm getting taller
And that my spellings getting better to
My scool report was good
I think you wood have been happy with it
I only have two more terms before I move to big scool
Bobby says that heel look after me
And hit anyone who trys to bully me
Bobby got in truble for hitting a boy who told him he woz a
loser cos he didn't have a dad
He has a very bad temper
Mummy just hugs him when hes cross
He carms down when she does that
But she cant be at the skool when he goes mad
Hes been better in the last 2 weeks
Hes got a girl friend – Sharma from next door
She comes round a lot and they snuggel playing Xbox games
together in the sitting room
Mummy is sad
Though Pete is here a lot
Mummy says he's a good friend
He trys to play with me
I wish it was you
Daddy, its been so long
Its cold outside this Chrissmas
I still sleep under your favrite coat cos it keeps me warm
I wish the coat was you
I feel protected under it
Which is good cos my tommy gun is broken
I'm looking after your favrite shoes

The one you wear indoors
I will give them to you when you come back home
I wunder where you are
And every day I think about wot you are doin
Do you miss us to
I wish you were here
Chrissmas is empty without you
Come home daddy
I luv you

Tommy xxxx

3. The Daughter

Even during the worst moments of his life, Jake had never imagined that he would be living rough at Christmas. Now reality had begun to bite as fiercely as the frost. He was on the run in Casino City from a man who wanted blood – *his* blood. He had a killer behind him and nothing in front of him except the ashen clouds which loomed ahead, heavy with their payload of snow.

After twenty minutes, Jake was exhausted. Drops of sweat were falling from his glistening brow. He winced as their salt began to sting his bloodshot, squinting eyes. He slowed down to a brisk walk, his already blistering feet leaving deep impressions in the thickening snow that layered the pavements from the riverside to the city centre. He had less than twenty-four hours to find a haven in an unfamiliar urban landscape – somewhere hidden from the predatory eyes of the Undertaker.

Jake considered his options as he walked past unlit, decorated store fronts with posters advertising winter sales, and then veered into meandering alleyways. He could find a homeless shelter, except that he knew this would be the first place he would plan to search if he was the hunter, not the hunted. He could knock on the doors of high-rise tenements and suburban homes, begging for somewhere to stay until he fell on better times and could recompense his hosts for their philanthropy. But who would ever trust a desperate stranger such as him on Christmas Day? Jake knew that he would never have opened his home for someone else. Why would anyone do the same for him?

He considered the police, but he also knew that no self-respecting officer would ever allow him to take refuge in a cell. He could imagine some firm but kindly duty sergeant. 'We are not in the practice of offering free bed and breakfast here, even at Christmas.'

For a moment Jake contemplated leaving the city, hailing a driver for a lift, but where would he go? He might find himself worse off than he was right now – roaming icy fields and country lanes with only the hope of some broken shack or dilapidated barn for shelter. That, he knew, meant probable death – and death was what he was trying to evade. No, Jake had run out of options and he knew it.

Turning the corner of a cobbled side street, Jake noticed a dark blue signboard outside an imposing red-bricked building. It read 'City Tabernacle' in antiquated, silver letters.

Above the stone-grey porch was draped a long white banner with the words 'King of Kings and Lord of Lords' printed in a royal purple colour, both ends punctuated by vivid images of golden crowns with many-coloured gems.

Two men, Jake guessed, were Africans were standing by the door in immaculate black suits and ties, concealed in part by overcoats with tiny sprigs of berried holly pinned into their lapels.

Jake saw their broad smiles breaking frequently into laughter as they clapped their gloved hands and joked about the snow, which from time to time they moved from the steps and sidewalk with shovels – singing snatches of unfamiliar but joyful songs as they worked.

The fugitive could sense warmth coming from the building, emanating from a huge lantern hanging from the ceiling of the foyer where hundreds of people were mingling, clasping leather-bound Bibles under their arms.

Jake was not a churchgoer. He was not even a believer. But he guessed that this was not the kind of church that he had known from his upbringing – formal, traditional, cold. He conjectured – rightly, as it happened – that this was the furthest removed from a church whose God is remote and whose worshippers are indifferent. Beneath the two words 'City Tabernacle' he had already spotted the word 'Pentecostal' and knew enough to deduce that this would not be the kind of service that he had once attended as a child.

Normally he would have passed these people by, casting them a cursory and suspicious glance, and walked away. Today, however, was a very different day and Jake's desperation was stronger than his cynicism. He needed shelter. He needed protection. He needed warmth.

Taking a deep breath, he walked towards the two men standing with their shovels by their side. Both men smiled at him.

'Good morning, brother,' they said, almost in unison.

'Hi,' Jake replied, as strong hands were placed in his.

'Are you visiting us from out of town?' one asked.

'Yes,' Jake replied.

'Well, you are most welcome, friend,' the older of the two said. 'There's no safer place than the Lord's House on Christmas Day.'

Jake shivered at the reference to safety but then thanked the man before climbing up the steps into the spacious, bustling foyer of the church. In front of him there was a wooden table with a notice saying, 'Welcome Desk'. A young, attractive African woman with spiked black hair and a dark blue dress greeted him as he walked on by to one of two stone staircases that wound their way towards an upper storey of the building. He chose the staircase on his right and made his way to the top.

He passed through the door and found himself in a balcony full of sturdy pews. Walking to the front, he peered over the edge and saw an auditorium larger than any theatre he had ever seen. Row upon row of dark oak pews seemed to move in ranks towards a raised platform at the front, littered by microphones and music stands, instruments and monitors. At the back of the stage, a pulpit stood above the entire room like a crow's nest on an ancient frigate, its ledges capped by an illuminated lectern which was being attended by a short, smartly dressed, elderly man who placed a glass of fresh water just out of sight. On either side of the pulpit there were more pews fixed to the back wall, clearly reserved for the choir, above which the flags of many nations hung like pinions on the rigging of a ship.

Jake sat for over an hour, watching as the stage began to fill with musicians and technicians. He saw about fifty men and women dressed in bright blue robes with white roughs ascend the stage and then up some steps into the stalls behind the pulpit, carrying music scores and big black Bibles bulging with note paper. They stood behind the platform with their arms at their sides, waiting quietly and reverently, like sailors on a parade. A woman in her forties took the stage and began to speak through a tiny microphone that had been fastened to her head and which protruded almost imperceptibly in front of her mouth. The choir brought their music sheets to their chests. The musicians donned their instruments. And within seconds, Jake was greeted by the rousing sound of many voices singing in impressive harmony, 'Joy to the world!'

For the next couple of hours, Jake sat or stood among a packed congregation. He estimated there were at least 1,000 people in the building, all of them participating with enthusiasm not only with the singing, but also with the prayers and even the announcements.

Jake had never imagined that laughter or tears belonged in church.

Nearly every uttered sentence seemed to be greeted by the sound of a sonorous 'Amen' from someone in the congregation. On one occasion Jake became mesmerised, as the words of a song – which had been projected onto two large screens each side of the stage – were removed as the congregation began to use a language he had never heard before, but which he sensed was spiritual. As he looked around, he saw that almost every arm was raised in adoration. Some were looking up at the gilded ceiling of the church as if they were communicating with a host of unseen visitors. Others seemed to be even more entranced, their eyes rolling upwards and backwards as they wept and sang in unintelligible words the music of their hearts.

As the songs continued, Jake found himself reacting with the swaying crowd, his feet making tiny movements in response to the enthusiastic clapping of the choristers and the hypnotic rhythm of the black musicians at the front, whose exceptional ability even Jake could not deny. When this sea of praise began to subside, Jake was surprised by how disappointed he felt. He wanted more. He longed for a new surge of adoration.

As he sat down, a chubby, cheerful woman – who turned out to be the Sunday school principal – came to the front and introduced a short drama involving some of the children. There followed a poignant and at times hilarious sketch. Three black boys acted the part of the wise men, travelling from Persia to Bethlehem, carrying gifts for the Saviour born in a manger – a real baby, as it happens, held by a young single mum who had given birth a month before, and who was sitting under a make-shift shelter to which the heavy-laden Magi were journeying at the front of church.

When the boys – dressed in ornate, bejewelled costumes – arrived at the manger, they laid their gifts at the feet of the mother, whose baby was now gurgling and cooing as she fed him at her breast. The first boy laid a fake bar of gold at the manger, clearly upset at letting go of his precious cargo. Many in the congregation nodded sympathetically at each other as they empathised with his reluctance.

The second boy sneezed violently while opening a bottle of expensive, pungent perfume, obliterating the word 'myrrh' in the process. As the mother wiped her face, the laughter began to grow as the child recoiled at the smell of the fragrance, covering his nose.

But the loudest laugh of all was reserved for the third boy, who had clearly lost the word 'frankincense' somewhere on his brief pilgrimage to the shelter, and proudly announced as he lifted his gift with exaggerated dignity, 'And this is Frankenstein.'

With that a tsunami of merriment broke from the audience upon the stage, followed by a resounding and united clap which morphed in turn into a lingering and heartfelt ovation. When the noise died down the young mum thanked the Magi, saying with an amplified voice, 'These gifts you bring in your hands mean everything. But greater still is the gift of adoration from your hearts. Thank you, great kings, for honouring the greater King.'

With that, the mother and child and the rest of the cast departed and the singers back of stage stood to attention. The musicians took their instruments, the conductor took the stage, and the choir began to sing an anthem.

Who are the wise men now, when all is told?
Not men of science; nor the great and strong;
Not those whose eager hands pile high the gold;
But those, amid the tumult and the throng,
Who follow still the Star of Bethlehem.

No sooner had the final chord reverberated than a tall, distinguished grey-haired man appeared in the pulpit to preach about the Magi, who had travelled over 800 miles on camels to meet the baby in Bethlehem. Jake thought his talk was eloquent and often humorous. He even caught himself on one occasion almost saying 'Amen' as the person on his right exclaimed, 'Preach it, pastor!' And the pastor did. He spoke with many stirring, personal anecdotes about the three stages of the wise men's search.

He talked about the first phase as the Star, explaining that the Magi were drawn to the manger by a supernatural sign in the skies, and that God had supernatural ways of drawing people towards his Son – both then and now.

He then moved to the second phase which he called the Scriptures. The wise men were told of the place of the nativity from King Herod's theologians, who pointed to an Old Testament Scripture that prophesied about the birth of the Messiah.

He finished with the fulfilment of man's religious quest, the Saviour, saying that everyone is on a spiritual journey of some kind or another, but that the end of all our seeking is to be found in an encounter with the Saviour of the World.

With that, the congregation began to clap. And they clapped even louder still when the suited pastor played his final card. 'Wise men sought Him long ago. Wise men and women do today.'

At that, the shouts and claps grew to a fervent crescendo which was accompanied by 'Hallelujahs' from the preacher, whose speaking now merged into singing. As his whooping grew, a Hammond organ began to play and before Jake knew it, the whole company of congregants was pouring out its heart in a storm of praise that rose and fell like great waves on the high seas.

When the last notes dissipated, the preacher descended the steps of the pulpit to the front of stage and everyone became quiet.

Earlier in the service a younger pastor had announced that today was a special gift day which the church had been preparing for during the month of December. Everyone had been encouraged to bring a financial gift that would go towards the funding of a homeless mission in the city. As a Christmas carol was sung, Jake watched as hundreds walked towards the front of church, leaving envelopes in large wicker baskets situated there. Hundreds of others had stood in line at terminals, waiting to give by credit card.

Minutes later, the elderly pastor stood at the front of the stage.

'As you know, today we've been collecting for our mission to the homeless in our city. We needed £150,000 to meet our target. You've seen the plans on the walls of our cafe in the basement. Well, I am here to tell you that we didn't manage to raise that sum.'

For a moment, there was a groan of disappointment.

'We managed to raise just over £250,000!'

As the final figure was announced, a thousand cheers went up. When they at last died down, the pastor spoke.

'This is a wonderful gesture. I'm so proud of you all. I know that this has involved great sacrifice. Thank you for being such an amazing, generous, and compassionate family.'

With that, he pronounced a blessing, asking everyone to be mindful of those who were abandoned or bereaved, lonely or estranged. He then wished everyone a happy Christmas and encouraged all those present to exchange a greeting with each other.

Straight away someone behind Jake poked him in the back. He swivelled round to see a boy with dark black hair, about the age of his younger son Tommy, reaching out his arms. Jake at first resisted, but the boy was insistent, thrusting both his hands towards the tall stranger in front of him, unwilling to yield until he had got his way.

Jake felt the tears begin to fill his eyes.

He leaned forward, gingerly at first, until he saw the unmistakable innocence of the young boy's gesture of affection. He bent down and hugged the child, who hung on tight with both his arms. Jake closed his eyes and the faces of his sons passed before him.

From that moment on, Jake was swamped by people lavishing him with Christmas greetings. Some shook him by the hand, but most took hold of him in their arms and embraced him before drawing back and saying, 'God bless you, friend.'

One elderly African lady, with a bright yellow hat and bright yellow shoes to match, hugged him and then took him by the hand and led him all the way to the basement of the church, where tables had been set with striped red and white cloths and green napkins. She sat him down and brought him freshly ground coffee and a chocolate biscuit, telling him he looked tired and thin and that he needed 'sustenance'.

Jake watched the people lining up at the coffee counter, taking their refreshments and then disappearing into the throng of people now milling in the room. After an hour, the space was almost empty. It was 1 p.m. and there were Christmas dinners to prepare and celebrate at home. By 2 p.m. Jake was the only person in the basement. The two old ladies serving coffee had locked up the hatch and bid him happy Christmas, telling him the church would be closing very soon but that he was welcome to return the following Sunday. Until then, they said, the building would be locked.

As Jake heard this, the seeds of an idea began to grow. If he concealed himself, he could shelter from the cold for the next five days. There might even be food and drink within the church's many rooms – 'sustenance' to keep him satisfied until the place was occupied by worshippers again. It was a gamble, but gambling was Jake's world.

Jake left the cafe area and walked down a cold and dusty corridor. At the end, there was a door whose white paint was peeling from just about every inch of its worn and faded frame. He leaned his shoulder against the wood and grasped the rusty latch. One firm shove and the door gave way, revealing a small storeroom with cardboard and plastic boxes piled high with hymn books, hassocks, robes and surpluses.

Jake took one quick glance around the darkened room and spied a hiding place. In the corner stood a six-foot plastic Christmas tree, resting on the floor, its base and trunk removed. Making his way past the boxes, Jake swept some straggling branches from his face and pushed himself behind the tree's fake foliage, keeping still and calming down his heart rate and his breathing. For ten minutes he remained motionless, before he heard footsteps approaching the door. A moment later the door swung open and a man peered in, sweeping the room with his eyes. 'That's the last room,' he shouted to an unseen companion behind him. 'Time to lock up and go home.'

The two men walked away, their footsteps disappearing into the cafe area and up the stairs. Jake breathed a sigh of relief and stood still for another ten minutes. Sharp green pine needles brushed against and tickled his face, tempting him to sneeze. But he kept himself in check, waiting until he sensed that everyone had gone and he was now alone.

There was no alarm system within the church, which Jake regarded as remarkable, so he explored the building from the basement to the gallery without any fear of discovery. There were many rooms. Some were used for offices and had computers and printers parked on crowded desks. Others were filled with tiny chairs and had children's paintings on their walls. To Jake's delight, one room that seemed to be the nerve centre of the Sunday school contained boxes of sweets and crisps in an unlocked wardrobe, whose lower drawers revealed cans of Coca Cola and other soda drinks.

Jake filled an empty plastic crate with supplies for several days. *Children's party fare*, he thought. *Not particularly healthy, but it is Christmas, and it's better than nothing.*

He carried his provisions from the room, making sure all lights were off, and looked for a safe place within the church where he could make his temporary home. Eventually he found it, but not where he had at first anticipated. Jake had imagined that the most promising place to bed down would be in one of the smaller rooms in one of the corridors leading from the auditorium. But he found it in the most open space of all – right at the front of the sanctuary.

From the balcony, he had earlier seen the shelter to which the three wise boys had come, bearing their gifts. To him, watching from above, it had looked like a bold attempt to create a Middle Eastern stable. But when he walked towards it at ground level he could now see that it was no such thing at all. Instead of troughs and animals there were sleeping bags with people lying in them – not real people, but dummies dressed as homeless men and women.

As soon as Jake realised this, he saw both the opportunity as well as the originality of what lay before him. He admired the way the church had made the Christmas story relevant. This was a shelter, yes, but it was a homeless shelter, and that spoke far more powerfully within a city than donkeys and oxen ever could.

At the same time Jake understood, with a heart made opportunistic by expediency, that he could make use of just about every item in the shelter if he had to resort to living on the streets, as now seemed more than probable. Everywhere he peered, Jake's eyes homed in on the contents of his survival kit. There were cardboard boxes and blankets, sleeping bags and pillows, canned food and water canteens, all strewn throughout the shelter. Even the straw, bin liners and old newspapers could come in handy. A shopping trolley from a local supermarket stood proudly at the back of the shelter, with several rugs that had certainly seen much better days crammed within its metal bars.

As the afternoon wore on and the light outside began to dim, Jake organised his bed and reshuffled the shopping cart. He emptied it before wedging several inches of old newspapers into the bottom of the trolley. On top of that he added straw before placing another inch or so of newspapers on top. Above these went the frayed blankets, plus the best sleeping bag Jake could find in the shelter, all of which acted as a mattress for some food and clothing he had foraged.

He then removed most of his clothes before trying on some garments from the male manikins. He found a pair of jeans, a

Forester's shirt, old trainers and a thick, tattered sweater which fitted well enough. He left his Armani suit, shirt and shoes under one of the sleeping bags in exchange for the cheaper items he had pilfered before placing his overcoat in the trolley and pushing it into the shadows at the rear of the shelter.

Having arranged his bedding, he tore into a bag of crisps and drank the contents of a soda can before eating half a bar of candy. After his hunger subsided, he started to prepare for a night's sleep. Forced by scarcity to improvise, he tried as best he could to clean his teeth with a mixture of his own saliva and some dextrous movements of his index finger, but his teeth still felt rough and grubby. He would have to make do.

The light had all but gone now, so he used a small torch from his phone to illuminate his surroundings. As Jake climbed into one of the sleeping bags and rested his head upon a pillow, he shone the torch from right to left, and up and down. He felt disoriented among the hollow, plastic men and women, their faces peering blankly, eyes wide open in the dark. He comforted himself with the thought that it would be hard if not impossible to spot him, either in the light of day or the dark of night, concealed as he was among these silent, soulless mannequins.

He turned off the light and recalled the single parent mother who had sat just three feet from where he now was lying, rocking her own baby while singing several verses of the carol 'Away in a Manger'. As he had looked her, he had seen the word *courage*. For a moment he thought of Sally, realising with a shock for the first time in a year that she was now a single parent, too. As he thought of her, he remembered his boys. *What would they be doing now?* He tried to imagine them by the fire at home, sitting with their mum in front of the television, watching a Christmas Day movie and eating homemade soup and cheesy bread.

He closed his eyes and became aware of the stillness in the stony, silent space in which he now was camping. The only sounds he could hear in the cavernous recesses of the building were the occasional moans of a gust of wintery wind outside and the intermittent noise of water passing through the antiquated pipes in the church.

As he manoeuvred his body into a position that afforded him at least some relief from the tiled floor, sleep at last overwhelmed him, the last image in his exhausted mind the boy behind him at the end of church, his arms stretched out towards him. His last thought before he went to sleep, *'That boy doesn't have a dad either.'*

It was twelve hours later that Jake awoke, his eyes weary and his body aching. He coughed several times, becoming aware of his own stale breath and the teeth he could not clean, at least not with a toothbrush and toothpaste.

He surveyed his surroundings once again and counted eight mannequins lying in the dormitory that he had joined. Four had women's wigs on, one which looked like the golden mullet of a rock star from the eighties. The other four were clearly meant to be male, although all the mannequins had faces with a genderless, robotic aura and the faintest hint of a smile which, in the cool light of day, looked less sinister than the night before, and yet still caused his tired heart to tremble.

Jake rose to his feet, stretching his limbs, before wandering through the auditorium past empty pews to a doorway at the back. He climbed some stairs and explored a corridor that he had missed the night before. The last room he navigated was a kitchenette that served a spacious open-plan office, whose desks were covered with discarded Christmas hats and unused crackers. In it Jake found a fridge and helped himself to an egg-based flan, topped with mature cheese and broccoli, which he heated in what looked like a first-generation microwave. He was hungry, hungrier than he could ever recall, so he wolfed down a crusty pie in a matter of seconds, washing it all down with water that he drank from the stubborn kitchen tap.

For the next four days, Monday to Thursday, Jake wandered throughout the church building, often walking with a blanket around his shoulders. His favourite room was the senior pastor's office. It was situated beyond the open-plan offices and the kitchenette, and protected by a smaller room where a secretary presumably sat at a reception desk. The senior pastor, as it turns out, was in fact a bishop. His title was engraved on a clean and shiny plaque on the door to the inner office, which Jake now entered. The first thing he saw was a six-foot long silver sword hanging in a wooden display case behind the bishop's expansive, imitation oak desk. On closer inspection, Jake saw that the sword was an emblem of office given by another, referred to in an inscription beneath the sword as 'the bishop of bishops' – his name engraved above the date and time on which this gift had been conferred.

Jake sat down behind the desk, looking out across the room at a long, burgundy leather sofa on his left, an identically coloured armchair on his right, and a glass coffee table between them, littered with church magazines, one of which had the bishop's face on the cover underneath the headline, 'Mercy Ministry in the Inner City'. He got up, walked to the bookshelves that lined every wall of the room, apart from the space behind the desk which was broken up by two latticed windows, whose ledges were adorned with framed photographs of the bishop and his wife and children.

He then perused the shelves, impressed by the bishop's range of reading – everything from volumes of theology, biblical studies and Greek and Hebrew lexicons to books about poverty, HIV/Aids, adoption, education, literature, and war and peace. This bishop was evidently a well-read man, a fact for which his unknown visitor was grateful in his four-day stay, as he thumbed through books in the daylight hours to stave away the tedium.

On one occasion, Jake opened the only item of furniture to interrupt the array of bookcases – an old wardrobe that seemed to climb all the way to the height of the ceiling. Inside he found the bishop's robes and a change of clothes – a perfectly tailored suit hanging next to five finely ironed shirts, all with sewn-in slips into which you could insert a dog collar. Some of the robes were festooned with bright green and yellow colours, betraying the bishop's African roots. Others were more sombre, one completely black, like a raven's wings, which Jake imagined was for funerals.

He closed both doors of the wardrobe until he heard the old spring mechanism click and he knew they were secure. He had touched nothing, impressed as he was by a sense of the sanctity of what he saw within. As he turned to his right towards the desk again, he noticed a pair of small wooden steps lying against the side of the armchair. He had never seen such a thing before, but he sensed what it was – a homemade kneeler where the bishop prayed. It was well worn from constant use and had evidently been repaired and strengthened many times, he imagined by a friendly handyman.

Jake loved this room, moved as he was by the atmosphere of serenity that seemed to linger like an unseen cloud of reassuring but indefinable presence. He spent many hours from early morning to early evening sitting quietly, reading deeply, looking at the family portraits on the windowsills, thinking of his own family back home, before falling asleep from time to time on the bishop's sofa.

By Thursday night he was beginning to feel the pressure of an intensifying ambiguity within his soul. He longed to stay within this sacred space, basking in the tranquillity that bathed his anxious mind like holy oil. At the same time, he knew that Sunday was imminent and that even on the Saturday the building might be busy once again, with administrators typing on computers and musicians practising on their instruments in preparation for sacred worship. He knew he couldn't stay beyond Friday evening at the latest and that even that might well be pushing it.

For Jake, the final and defining spur to act occurred on Thursday night.

He had tucked himself up in his sleeping bag in the shelter in the sanctuary, and was sucking on a strawberry lollipop which he had found within a cupboard in the Sunday school room. He was on the edge of drifting into a deep sleep when he heard footsteps on the staircase leading to one of the doorways into the auditorium. As he peered towards the back of the hall, he saw the shadowy outline of two adults holding hands as they walked towards the shelter, one of them carrying a Victorian gas lamp.

Jake tucked his head beneath the top of his sleeping bag and kept completely still from head to toe as the two figures approached the entrance of the shelter. Just as he was sure he was going to be discovered, the two strangers veered away and moved towards the stage. They climbed some steps before kneeling underneath a dark brown, humble wooden cross just to the right of the stage, fixed to the wall, directly within Jake's eye level.

One of them placed the burning light of the lamp beneath the cross and then bowed their head. Jake heard both the voices which resonated from the other side of the room. One he recognised straightaway as that of the bishop. The other belonged to a woman, and from their obvious intimacy Jake guessed that this was the bishop's wife. They were praying together, their voices sometimes speaking separately and at other times merging like converging melodies into a single, heartfelt utterance.

Jake could only make out snippets of what they said as the flame within the lantern seemed to dance in response to the tone and content of their supplications: references to orphans and to widows; to the poor and the oppressed; to the bereaved; to young and troubled teens; to individual names like 'Frank' and 'Barbara'; to the city; to revival; to the homeless and to the mission they were setting up. In all of this, they kept addressing the one to whom they prayed as their 'heavenly Father', sometimes even calling him 'Papa' and 'Dad', as their prayers ascended in passionate and tearful crescendos before falling into almost imperceptible whispering.

For several hours, the bishop and his wife continued praying until their heartfelt words and resounding sighs ran out.

The two now embraced the silence like an old friend, tilting their heads towards each other until the bishop's wife was leaning on her husband's shoulder, warming her hands at the glowing, bulbous base of the antique lantern.

After several minutes, the bishop moved his head towards hers and kissed her gently on the top of her head, before taking her hand in his as he stood up, gathering the lamp in his other hand. He turned up the heat for a moment and as the brilliant flame increased within, the two of them spoke in perfect unison. 'The fire must be kept burning on the altar day and night.' With that, they both descended from the stage, unaware of the silent witness to all their invocations.

As the two of them prepared to leave the auditorium, Jake looked up and out towards them. They paused as he peered at them. And as they did, the bishop raised his hand towards the shelter, as if to bless it.

Jake froze within its unseen recesses, his face locked in the wide-eyed stare of the empty mannequins around him. A second later, the bishop and his soulmate had turned around and left, the sound of their footsteps falling away as they walked from the stone floor of the foyer to the porch and left the tabernacle.

<hr />

Jake slept fitfully that night, tossing and turning on his mattress made of straw and his bedsheets made of dirty newspapers. He woke at inconsistent intervals as his restless soul shot questions to the surface of his mind like detonating fireworks. *Why did the bishop turn? Did he see me? What was he doing when he raised his hand towards the shelter? Was he waving? Was he blessing me?*

As Jake came to full consciousness at daybreak, he lay on his side, looking at a female mannequin who was staring past his shoulder towards the stage.

'Time to leave,' he said to her, as he lifted himself to a seated position and looked behind him at his shopping cart, packed like a deck of old cards.

'I'll make one last sweep of the building before dark and then I'm out of here.'

Jake spent the morning in the bishop's office, reading a short book that the bishop had himself written about the Christmas story, called 'Danger in the Manger'. It was a political interpretation of the story of Christ's birth, written in a popular style, but with a strong political message of compassion for the powerless.

After lunch, Jake searched the building from top to bottom and acquired several new items for his trolley – sticky tape, a pair of scissors, a woollen hat, some gloves and a thick scarf.

By 6 p.m., the church was shrouded in thick darkness once again. He could not take the chance that someone would visit the auditorium for cleaning or for choir practice, so he pushed his overflowing trolley to the back of the great chamber – its wheels nosily betraying their reluctance – and passed through the sanctuary doors. He ferried his cargo through the foyer to the entrance of the church, unlocked the Yale lock of the glass front door, before navigating his cart onto the icy, stone steps outside, rolling down a ramp designed for wheelchairs.

Jake was about to turn a corner onto another street when he cast a cursory look over his left shoulder towards the City Tabernacle, his refuge for the last five days. He paused for a moment, taking in the dimly lit façade of the brick building. It was then that he saw them. They must have been there all along, but he had been too distracted to notice.

There, looking down from a stone ledge just beneath the roof, were the statues of two angels, looking down at all who left and entered the tabernacle. They seemed to stare at him, their arms outstretched beneath enfolding wings as if pleading, their melancholy eyes frozen in a look of unending mercy.

Jake's heart melted under their gaze. 'I'm sorry for stealing these things,' he said. 'One day I will repay you.'

He swung round and strode off towards the city centre, keeping always to alleyways and side streets. After four hours of walking in and out of shadowy cul-de-sacs and entrances, he found a dead-end street filled with skips, wheelie bins and broken beer bottles. He pushed his cart to the end of the short street where a tall brick wall stopped him in his tracks, its summit protected by some barbed wire and broken glass. He cleared a space in one corner at the bottom of the wall and emptied his trolley until he found his cardboard, newspapers and straw. He created a thick layer of cardboard first. He then took four heaps of straw and placed them on the cardboard, roughly the length and width of his supine body. He then placed newspaper over the straw before putting his sleeping bag on top of that, with three blankets. He positioned the shopping cart beside his makeshift bed and lay it on its side, creating the beginnings of a partition to protect him from the chilly wind. To this he added cardboard, which not only bolstered his defence against the icy gusts that blew without warning down the street, but also acted as a temporary roof.

Jake's fingers were now turning blue within his gloves. He drank some Coca Cola and ate two bars of chocolate before bedding down.

Once inside his sleeping bag, he drew his blankets up and brought the cardboard roofing down. Even with his woollen hat and gloves, his thick sweater and socks, his overcoat and scarf, he still shivered violently, wondering to himself how anyone survived the winter months in a hinterland like this. By one o'clock in the morning, Jake was feeling colder than he could ever remember. He thought to himself, *This is it. I'm going to die. There's no way I'm going to see daybreak.*

Just as he was about to yield to the numbing cold, he sensed something wet snuffling around his head and then all over his face. *This is it,* Jake thought. *Game over.*

But the game wasn't over. It was only when Jake felt thin, long whiskers brushing against his cheeks, tickling his skin, that he began to realise what it was. The sound of sniffing was the final giveaway, as was a warm, rough tongue that dragged across his icy cheeks. It was a large, stray dog – a German Shepherd – that had sought and found some warmth on a bitter night.

Jake opened up the top of his sleeping bag and unzipped the edge, offering his canine friend the opportunity of shelter. The dog, desperate to get warm, clambered inside head first, before turning somewhere about Jake's waist and returning with its dribbling nose to the top again.

Jake drew the blankets and the cardboard back above him. Within seconds he began to benefit from the warm body. There they lay without moving, drawing strength and comfort from each other's body heat, until the blackened firmament turned leaden grey and the first hint of a morning sky began to appear above them.

Jake woke first to find the dog nestled into the scarf around his neck, her long and bony back pressed close into his stomach, her tail down to his shins. He looked at her eyes, which were still closed tight. She looked old and weary. A large scar extended from just above her left eye towards her tall and pointed left ear. When she opened her eyes as Jake began to stir, he saw that the pupil of this eye was damaged too, and what looked like a thin and milky membrane had drawn itself like a curtain over her tired retina.

'Hello,' said Jake.

The German Shepherd squinted as he spoke, drawing her face into what looked like the makings of a canine smile. This was confirmed by the dog's long tail wagging against his legs beneath in the folds of the sleeping bag.

Jake reached out into his capsized trolley, groping for a packet of biscuits or some crisps. Withdrawing a red bag, he tore open the top with his stained teeth before removing a few crisps in his hands. The German Shepherd lifted her head, her ears pricking, and started sniffing vigorously at the edge of the bag.

'Oh no you don't,' Jake said, fearing that the dog would do to the crisp bag what she had done to his sleeping bag the night before.

He pushed her eager nose away and held two crisps in his cold fingers before her face. She leaned her head to one side and took the food from his hands without touching his fingers at all, crunching it before swallowing. No sooner had she done this than she began to stare at the crisps once more, moving her hungry eyes from the bag to Jake and back again, her brown and black ears at full stretch and maximum anticipation, her chops revealing a thin layer of white saliva.

'Oh, go on then,' Jake said, tipping the whole bag onto some cardboard just beyond her face, watching as she consumed the larger pieces before licking every tiny fragment she could find.

'I'll call you Sandy,' he said, 'because you kept me warm last night.'

For the next four months, Jake and Sandy went everywhere together. They learned where food and drink could be found. Jake plundered the bins and skips behind grocery stores and supermarkets, rescuing food that was still in its packaging, untouched and perfectly edible, but past the official sell-by date. He and his friend lived off everything from prawn mayonnaise sandwiches to smoked salmon, filling their empty stomachs with anything that gave them 'sustenance'.

In the early hours of the morning they would go to restaurants and rummage in their back yards, Jake taking the residue of wine and spirits from discarded bottles, creating full ones out of nearly empty ones. These he would consume late at night whenever he began to feel the cold. The alcohol would cause his body temperature to rise, always making him feel warmer.

In all of this, Jake and Sandy kept themselves to themselves, never settling in the popular places where other homeless people slept, rarely talking to other wanderers on the streets. They avoided the heated entrances to shopping centres and especially the warm recesses of underground car parks – all of which might well have given them greater comfort, but at the same time greater exposure to the eyes of the Undertaker.

Jake and Sandy kept moving with their trolley from one secluded alleyway to another, creating temporary shelters behind anything large enough to conceal their cardboard camp, sleeping with one eye open, prepared for anything.

As the evenings were beginning to get lighter and warmer, Jake began to feel as if his life was bearable despite his often hostile and inclement circumstances. He had a faithful friend in Sandy. He still had his trolley with all its contents. He knew where to find food and drink. He had maintained his independence. He had kept low, avoiding the searching eyes of predators. He had not been beaten up. He was becoming streetwise. And there was a hint of springtime in the air.

———

Just at the very moment when the knots of despair were being massaged from his heart, Jake's world collapsed like a house of cards.

One night in April, Jake had fallen into a deep sleep in the daytime. He was sitting upright on the doorstep of a disused house. Sandy was lying with her head beneath his chin, her body lying on his torso.

It was Sandy who saw them first – four young leery looking men in hooded sweatshirts, climbing over a wall further down the side street and walking on tiptoe towards them. Sandy barked as they approached the shopping cart which Jake had, on this one occasion, allowed to stand unguarded. The young men grabbed the trolley as Sandy jumped out of the sleeping bag, her lips unfurled, her teeth bared and the hackle raised on her back.

The youths set off at speed, pushing the uncoordinated trolley as they sprinted towards the entrance to a muddy pitch with dirty white football posts, the shopping cart lurching wildly in front of them. Sandy ran after them as Jake awoke and immediately launched himself in hot pursuit of his dog, shouting at her to 'get 'em, girl' as she chased them round a wall into the park out of Jake's field of vision. But Sandy could not hear. As she had cantered round the end of the wall, two of the men had been waiting for her. One of them drew a short metal pipe from underneath his sweatshirt, the other a blade from a leather scabbard which was attached to his belt and hidden from view.

As Sandy turned from the street to the park, one of the men brought the bar down upon her skull, fracturing it instantly. The other thrust his blade into her heart.

Jake heard the yelp and shuddered. He called out Sandy's name, begging her to come back, telling her that the trolley didn't matter.

But it was too late.

When Jake passed the edge of the wall he saw her, lying on her right flank, her head caved in, her brown and black fur matted with blood. Her good eye was lifeless, staring at the sky.

Jake stroked her shoulders, pinching them from time to time, hoping that would bring her back but knowing that his friend was now beyond all hope, her life blood mingling with the mud.

As Jake looked up, he saw the men now carrying the trolley in the distance, laughing and shouting as they ran. From deep within the caverns of his stomach, a primal howl began to grow and grow until Jake's lungs were venting sounds he had never heard before. He roared one single word at the men. 'Bastards!'

He placed his hand upon Sandy's head and uttered words that he had heard from Father Jim when he had sat at the side of Sandra's lifeless corpse at the mortuary. 'Rest in peace,' he said, his voice cracking. 'Rest in peace,' he said again, while closing Sandy's open eye and leaning down to kiss her on the nose, still wet from the chase.

Jake stood to his feet and walked back from the playing field to the street, his eyes red with weeping and his throat sore from shouting. As he turned past the wall, his feet were momentarily caught within the folds of something lying on the pavement. It was his overcoat, which had always lain on top of the shopping cart, and which must have worked its way loose in the intense tumbling to which it had been subjected.

Jake picked it up and put it on over his sweater, brushing the dust off its front, thrusting his hands into its deep pockets.

'Thank you, Sandy,' he whispered into the wind as he turned his head in the direction of his dog. 'Your chase was not in vain.'

And yet Jake knew that it might as well have been. His trolley, with nearly all its contents, was now gone.

For a quarter of a year, it had been for him a mobile home. Now all he had was what he was wearing – and that was not nearly enough for him to survive.

For the next two weeks, Jake wandered desperately on the streets by night, sleeping under a large weeping willow tree beside a canal by day, using a discarded sleeping bag and mud-caked rugs – the final legacy of a lonely vagrant Jake would never meet but whose odour lived on in the tartan inlay of the sleeping bag.

Jake embraced this solitude until one night he decided to go out foraging for food in an unexplored estate in the red-light district of the city. There he found three homeless men at the end of a street that ran adjacent to a condemned and unoccupied building – a colourless high-rise block of stone, covered by blue cladding, a gigantic eyesore that the council had built half a century before to accommodate a forgotten underclass. Its stairwells were disfigured by obscene and angry messages, spray-painted with livid aerosols. Its long-abandoned elevators stank of stale urine and its doors were either hanging off their hinges or removed altogether.

Jake made his way to the three figures standing around a burning oil drum. They were warming their hands and toasting pieces of meat retrieved from unopened supermarket packets from a recently built superstore a mile outside the city limits. Jake moved to the fire and stretched his gloved hands into the gusts of heat that were blowing towards him in reviving bellows. He looked down to begin with at his feet, choosing not to engage with the bearded men, who were thrusting their food into the fire. As he continued to look down, Jake caught the reflection of his face in a puddle. For a moment, he was shocked. He was looking at a man with long and unkempt hair, a bushy greying beard, exhausted eyes, stained teeth and what looked like skid marks on his sallow, bony cheeks. This brought him short. He was no different from these men. They were all of them just gloomy, empty, lifeless habitations – doomed for demolition like the grubby, hollow tenements that overshadowed them.

'Mind if I join you?' Jake enquired, in a voice that betrayed that he really did not care if they answered either way.

'No, we don't,' one of the men replied.

'Been on the streets long?' another man asked.

'Since Christmas Day.'

The men nodded. One of them pushed a thin, metal skewer with a large piece of toasted beef towards Jake, who took it and chewed it.

'Thank you,' Jake said.

For the next hour, he stood beside the flames that rose and fell from deep within the iron drum. Three women in fake fur coats, whom Jake deduced were 'painted ladies', came and stood with them to warm their hands, until a black saloon drew up, a window lowered, and a dark-skinned pimp shouted at them to move along and get to work.

'All right, Daddy, all right,' one of them replied. 'We're leaving.'

'Get a move on, then,' the suited man replied. 'Time is money.'

The girls moved off but the car remained. The pimp, whose padded shoulders were heavily laden with golden chains and necklaces – including a standout cross with sparkling jewels engraved within its centre – turned his attention to the three men the other side of the fire from Jake.

'Come here, you,' the pimp said in a commanding voice, pointing his finger towards the man in the middle.

The man walked round the drum towards the car. For several minutes, the two of them engaged in a heated conversation, the pimp issuing warnings and threats, his bedraggled companion offering excuses, cowering at times like a frightened animal. Jake heard the words 'tomorrow or else', before the pimp slipped back into the dark interior of his limo and the electric window rose to terminate the interchange between them.

The car drove off and the man returned, looking shaken. He reached inside a pocket of his overcoat and took a long, fat joint from its folds. Using a stick, whose end he lit from the oil drum fire, he ignited his bulging, home-made cigarette and inhaled, blowing puffs of smoke into the night air, smiling with relief.

'That stuff will be the death of you,' one of his companions said. But the man did not hear, or if he did, he did not care.

'I'm getting my head down,' the third man said.

'Me too,' another replied.

'Are you coming?' one of them asked Jake. Jake nodded and followed the three men as they picked up shoulder bags and tattered suitcases and walked towards the pallid high-rise block.

Once inside, Jake walked behind them as they shuffled like prisoners up one flight of stairs after another until they reached the top – 'the Penthouse Suite', as one described it – an empty apartment with bedding on the floor around the edges of its one main room, and the burned out remains of a fire on the stone floor in its centre.

A fresh fire was lit there, along with another joint, before the men began to settle. Jake was given a mattress just inside the doorway to the room, with the explanation that its owner had been rushed to hospital with a fatal cardiac arrest because he mixed vodka with the medication he was taking for his heroin addiction.

'It's the 'feller' who makes you do that,' one of them had said.

'What feller?' Jake replied.

'Old Nick, the Devil,' he said. 'You've got to watch your back all the time.'

'Enough of that,' one of the men said. 'It's not safe to mention his name. Cheer us up with some of your music.'

With that, the man who had referred to 'the feller' drew an old silver flute from his coat.

'You're in for a treat,' said the man who had requested the music. 'Our friend here used to be a professional. Played in orchestras, he did. He travelled all over the world, on famous stages, in front of big crowds.'

'Until the feller got me,' the musician interjected.

'What do you mean?' Jake asked.

'I couldn't cope anymore,' the man replied, moving the reed of the flute close to his lips. 'I couldn't cope anymore.'

'What with?'

'The great contradiction.'

The man could see that Jake needed further explanation.

'The contradiction between the ugliness of the world and the beauty of the music I was playing.'

'Why do you keep playing, if you feel like that?' Jake asked as he saw the man place the tip of the reed to his lips.

'My notes are my last protest against the darkness,' the man said.

As the musician began to clear the flute with strong breaths through the lip plate, Jake began to imagine what melody was possible from such a dented, stained instrument.

Jake watched as the man placed the crown to his lips and began to express his angst in sequences of sounds which rose and fell like the dancing flames in the centre of the room. Sometimes he played familiar riffs; at other times, he poured out cadences that he composed in the moment.

As the mournful music went on, the man closed his eyes, leaned back ever so slightly, raised his gaze towards the heavens, and seemed to weep as his hands moved up and down the keys upon the silver barrel.

Jake's eyes grew heavy. He lay down and arranged the blankets to cover his body. His feet, stretched out towards the flames, were warm now. When the music finished, he listened to the crackling of the wood and smelled the lingering fragrance of the cigarette, whose incense for a little while disguised the rancid odours of the flat.

That night Jake dreamed, as he so often had since leaving home.

This time he saw himself outside a detached house in a suburban neighbourhood. It was not a home he recognised – certainly not his home.

The front door opened and a man walked out. He was in his early forties and he was limping. He looked in pain and he was holding his right hand tightly to his chest. His left hand was clasping two yellow ribbons. Standing within a few feet of Jake's face, he began to speak breathlessly.

'I have a message for you to give to someone. Will you do that for me?' Jake nodded his head. 'Tell her that I love her. Tell her that my heart is still hurting but that she has the power to change that. She knows what to do. Tell her it's time. It's time for all this pain to end. It's time for the homecoming to begin.'

As the man finished speaking, his face began to relax. He removed his hand from his heart and turned around to walk without a limp towards the house. As he neared the door, the building in front of him began to change into a gabled country house, its porch throbbing with a golden light that seeped from every crack around its doorframe.

As the man was about to walk in, he turned his head towards Jake one more time. 'Tell Christine that her father's mansion has many rooms,' he said with a broad smile. With that, the door opened wide, the golden light flooded out to meet him, and the man's outline merged with its pulsating brilliance until both he and it were one, and both were gone.

The next day, Jake woke feeling more refreshed than he had done for many weeks. Maybe it was the healing sound of music the night before, or the power of the light that he had seen in his dream, but that morning he sensed a warm serenity washing over his soul like a reviving shower.

As light began to pour through the cracked boards of the windows in the grimy apartment, Jake lay on his sleeping bag, looking around his dormitory. The charred remains of the fire lay in the centre of a room whose edges were hugged by bearded men in woollen hats. They were tucked into sleeping bags that now seemed to be extensions of their bodies, as motionless as cocoons in the litter layer of an impenetrable forest.

Jake spent the day with his three new companions, foraging for food and drink, from time to time engaging with the flautist who had mesmerised his heart.

'Are there many people like you on the streets?' Jake had enquired, after the four of them had fended off some feral youngsters.

'Yes,' the musician replied. 'There are many reasons why people turn to the streets. Some just want to opt out of the system, not having to pay water and gas bills and so on. Some have gone home to find that their key doesn't fit the lock and that those indoors don't want them anymore. Some find themselves in a situation they just can't deal with – maybe a death in the family, the loss of a job, or a husband or wife walking out. Some are just highly sensitive, often artistic people whose eyes have seen beyond the thin veil of superficiality which protects us from the darkness.'

'Like you, you mean,' Jake interrupted.

'I suppose so. You'd be surprised how many painters, poets, musicians, storytellers and philosophers there are living on the streets. Most people in conventional life think of us all as uneducated losers and treat us worse than dogs. But the truth is there is very little that separates us from them.'

'So, what was it that brought you here?'

'I saw too much,' he replied.

And that was it. Nothing more was said until the night drew in and the four of them were once again in their high-rise flat, crouching round the flickering flames of a fire fed by the wood from yet another door in the building.

'I won't play tonight,' the flautist said.

'Why?' Jake asked.

'The feller is abroad tonight.'

The musician crawled as deep as he could within his sleeping bag, which seemed to wrap itself automatically around him, easily conforming itself to the contours of his body. The dormitory grew quiet as the flames began to diminish and the light faded.

Jake took several hours to fall asleep, but when he did it was neither a deep nor an easy one. This night it was not his possessions he was watching, as so often had been the case before. Tonight it was something different, a sense of menace lurking in the shadows, of unseen dangers in the creaking nooks and crannies of the echoing building.

At three o'clock in the morning, Jake woke with a start. The door to the room they occupied was being slowly but perceptibly pushed. As it opened exactly half way, Jake could see from the light of the glowing embers of the fire that a tall man dressed in black with a balaclava over his head was leaning into the room. He was carrying a gun with a silencer on it in his left hand.

Jake froze with fear. Had the Undertaker discovered his high-rise hiding place? Was it time for him to pay the price for all his foolishness? The interloper switched on a low-lit torch in his right hand, shining it at Jake, whose eyes were now shut, before moving its beams beyond him to the man lying next to him.

Jake partially opened his eyes to see the man raise his gun. His heart began to beat so hard that he became convinced its thumping was now audible.

Is this it? he thought.

Jake heard the muted gun discharge. But the bullet missed him. It hissed just a matter of inches above his body and travelled at unimaginable speed beyond him, towards the man who two nights before had argued with the pimp in a black sedan.

The assassin had not come for Jake. He had come for the drug addict lying about two metres to his left, whose temple was now punctured by a small, dark hole leaking blood, his eyes and mouth open in a look of surprise.

As the man and his gun withdrew from the room, Jake's brow was wet and his mouth was dry. The black-clad stranger left as silently as he had arrived, disappearing from the room, the floor and the building with grim efficiency.

Jake sat bolt upright, trying to wake the other two men with words that were obscured and disrupted by involuntary gasps of air.

'What's the matter?' one of them asked.

Jake could not speak. He could only point at the body next to him. One of the men shuffled over in his sleeping bag.

'He's been shot,' he said. 'I told him those drugs would be the death of him.'

'And I told all of you the feller was up to no good tonight,' the flautist added.

'I… I… I can't stay here,' Jake stuttered.

Jake shook the bedding off his waist and somehow managed to stand. As he groped towards the door, he failed to hear the loud protestations of his two companions. He ran to the entrance of the apartment and beyond it to the stinking stairwell. He descended one floor after another until he found himself outside, taking deep gulps of night air, resting his hands upon his knees for a moment as he threw up on the pavement between his feet.

Jake pulled himself upright again and began to stride away from the high-rise flats as fast and as far as possible. He returned to being a wandering creature of the night, sleeping by day under thick bushes by the city canal, foraging by night, alert and hungry. For days, he lived and slept away from the crowds, a solitary and restless outsider. On one occasion, he saw a black hearse in the periphery of his vision, gliding slowly over a bridge across the canal where he was hiding. Panic gripped his heart as he thought of the Undertaker, propelling him to change his location once again.

Jake had never felt so alone before, and he continued to feel alone, until one night in the early onset of autumn everything changed when he met one of the girls living rough – a fellow loner called Christine.

He first saw Christine standing at the corner of an empty street, talking in an animated way to no one in particular. She was about nineteen and had been eking out an existence on the streets since she was ten.

When Jake saw her, it was well past midnight on a mild evening. She was wearing a dusky German army greatcoat with torn, red lapels and faded golden pips, two on her left shoulder, three on her right. She wore thick slate-coloured socks up to her shins and a pair of red corduroy trousers which picked up the colour of her lapels. Even her raven hair joined in with this unlikely integration of colours, matching the black army boots on her feet.

'Hello,' Jake said.

Christine turned away from Jake, and spoke to an invisible companion next to her.

'Should I speak to him?' she asked. She then turned to Jake and said, 'He says it's okay. My name is Christine. What's yours?'

'Jake.'

'How long have you been living rough?'

'Since Christmas Day,' Jake replied.

'Marriage breakdown?'

'Yes.'

He paused and lowered his gaze to the concrete. A sweet wrapper moved by a gust of wind stuck fleetingly to his ragged, faded trainers before passing on in random, sudden jerks down the wet pavement.

Jake pulled himself together and looked up. As he did, he looked at the girl, who had swivelled round to her unseen escort and was beginning to engage with him again.

'Wait a minute,' Jake said. 'Did you say your name was Christine?'

'Yes,' she replied. 'Why?'

'I had a dream two nights ago in which a dad told me to give a message to his daughter Christine. I think it might have been for you.'

'Tell me,' Christine replied. 'Tell me,' she repeated, pulling the sleeve of Jake's overcoat.

Jake narrated what he had seen and heard in his dream and, as he did so, Christine's face began to change from curiosity to melancholy.

'I've been waiting a long time to hear those words,' she said, sighing.

'What's the story?' Jake asked.

'It's a long one, like yours,' Christine replied.

'I've got all the time in the world,' Jake said. 'Please tell me… that is, if your friend thinks it's okay.'

Christine smiled before turning to her invisible companion once again. 'He says it's fine,' she said. 'I can trust you,' she added.

'How do you know?'

'Because my dad would never have appeared to you in a dream if he hadn't felt you were safe. Come on, let's go and get a coffee.'

Christine took hold of Jake's arm and started to walk him down a street towards a cafe run by a nearby church, where down-and-outs were offered hot drinks for free. Sitting opposite each other with a mug of coffee, Christine began to speak.

'It happened on the day of my tenth birthday,' she began, her voice lowering so no one could overhear. 'My dad and I were close, really close. The earliest memories I have are of him sitting me on his knee and pretending to be a horse. "Clippety-clop, clippety-clop, clippety-clop," he would say, over and over again, while lifting me gently up and down in perfect time with his impression of a horse's hooves. I adored it. I felt protected and exhilarated all at the same time. Every time he stopped and it was time for me to get off his knee, he would lean forward and kiss me on the back of my head and tell me that he loved me. I'll never forget it. Ever…'

Christine's eyes began to glisten.

'He loved taking me out on Daddy-daughter days to play zones and family restaurants. He showed me how to tie my hair and used to put yellow ribbons in my pigtails. He was my world, and I was his. I was his only daughter... and he used to joke, "You're Daddy's girl, but don't tell anyone I said that, especially your mum!"'

'What happened?' Jake whispered.

'Dad came home from work on my tenth birthday. He had promised to take me out to a Disney film and then on to my favourite pizza restaurant, just the two of us. He gave me a hug in the hallway the moment he entered the front door after work. I was always waiting for him.'

Christine took a sip from her coffee.

'He kissed me and said, "Double figures, gorgeous. Double figures! A few more years and you'll take the world by storm. I'm so proud of you."'

Christine coughed.

'Those were the last words he ever spoke to me. He walked up the stairs, pulling himself up using the banister. He looked more pale and tired than usual and I noticed that he was finding it hard to breathe, but I put that down to his asthma. I called up, "Daddy, are you okay?" But he didn't answer me. It was the only time I can ever remember him not answering me when I called.'

'Oh no,' Jake sighed, sensing already what he was about to be told.

'Later I learned from my mother he had gone into their bedroom and sat down in the armchair next to my mum's dressing table. This was where he had always used to sit and read me bedtime stories. He had been there only a few moments when he uttered a very deep sigh and just bowed his head upon his chest.'

She paused.

'And he left us. There had been no warnings. His heart gave out. And my world caved in.'

Christine's voice was a whisper now. 'All I remember was my mother screaming and me running up the stairs. I remember looking at the clock at the top of the stairs and noticing that it was exactly 6 p.m. Time seemed to freeze at that moment. I just knew that something awful had happened.'

Christine took another gulp of coffee. 'When I ran into the bedroom, I saw him there. Mum was feeling his pulse and shaking her head in despair. "He's gone!" she shouted. And he had gone. He'd gone forever. One moment I was getting into my prettiest, pink party dress to go out for a meal and a movie. The next moment men in black were round our house and putting my dad in a coffin.'

'I'm so sorry,' Jake said.

'That's okay.'

'Is that why you're on the streets?'

'Later that night I packed a small schoolbag with some clothes, a torch and food. I put on my trainers and my coat and walked out into the darkness. My house no longer felt like home. Dad was my safe place and he was gone. I just knew I'd never come back. Things between me and mum… well, let's just say they were very strained.'

'I get that,' Jake interrupted.

'Since then I've been living rough on the streets. Cardboard boxes, newspapers and shelters have been my home. When I sleep, and I don't ever sleep like I used to as a child, I often dream of him. I see him sometimes, walking towards me through a thick mist, calling out my name, reaching out with his hands, those lovely hands. They are always holding yellow ribbons. And every time I see him, he is trying to tell me something. But just as I'm about to hear him, I wake up.'

A tear ran down Christine's face. 'I have always wanted to know what he was trying to tell me… until now.'

Jake reached out and held Christine's hand and as he did, he began to recite again the words he had heard the father speak in his dream.

'Tell her that I love her. Tell her that my heart is still hurting but that she has the power to change that. She knows what to do. Tell her it's time. It's time for all this pain to end. It's time for the homecoming to begin.'

The two of them sat for a moment before Christine turned to her left and addressed an empty chair. 'That's what we've been waiting to hear, isn't it, Gusto?'

As she turned her face back to his, Jake noticed the rivulets her tears had made down the cheeks made rosy by the warm cafe.

'Can I ask you a question?' he asked.

'Depends what it is.'

'Well, it's just that you keep talking to someone that I can't see. Who are you speaking to? Is it your Dad?'

Christine smiled. 'It's Gusto.'

'Who's Gusto?'

'Gusto is my invisible friend. I've had him since I was a child.'

'That's a bit weird.'

'Not really. My dad used to say that everything I did, I did with gusto. I assumed that gusto was an unseen companion, so I started to talk to him every day. And I still do. I guess it connects me with my father.'

'That's cute,' Jake said.

'It's more than just cute. It's been a life-saver for me on the streets. They can be brutal for a girl like me. For anyone, in fact.'

'How have you survived?'

'By learning to be streetwise. I know where dangers lurk and I've just become alert to them. And on those occasions when others have tried to rob and mug me, or worse, Gusto and I have always managed to escape.'

'I could do with a bit of your gusto,' Jake interjected.

'Why's that?'

'Someone's after me. Someone who wants blood, someone who won't rest until I'm lying in a gutter with a bullet in my temple.'

'Tell me more,' Christine said.

Jake told her about his meeting with Pete and his descent into a world of gambling, his Christmas Eve rant at Sally and his exodus, his arrival in Casino City and his relationship with Sandra, his good fortune at the poker tables and his nemesis at the hands of the Undertaker. Jake held nothing back.

When he had finished, Christine stared into his eyes.

'You must miss your boys,' she said.

'I do,' Jake stuttered.

'I know for sure that they'll be missing you,' she added.

'I think they'll be too angry to miss me.'

'They will be angry, yes. But underneath the anger, there will be something far stronger and more hopeful – an ache. A tummy ache, only deeper - I call it a 'daddy ache'. Don't underestimate this, Jake. You're still their dad and they'd rather have a fallen father than no father at all.'

'I don't know,' Jake replied. 'I just can't believe that after all the anger there could be reconciliation.'

'But there can be. Even the most broken bridges can eventually be rebuilt.'

'I wish that was true,' Jake sighed.

'All things are possible,' Christine said. 'At least you're still alive.'

She turned her face away from Jake towards her invisible friend again. Jake was aware of a brief and whispered interchange between them before Christine turned to him.

'Look,' she said. 'You've done me a good turn by sharing your dream with me. I'd like to do you a good turn, too. You clearly need somewhere safe. I've got a place that no one knows about, a place where Gusto and I have been holed up for nearly two years. There's enough room for you as well. It's not five-star accommodation but it is a good hiding place.' Christine paused. 'Interested?'

'Yes,' Jake replied.

'Let's go then,' Christine said, putting her mug down on the table.

With that, the three of them left the cafe and strolled out into the night, Christine leading the way through secret side streets and arcane alleyways until they arrived at a broken brick wall, which Christine negotiated in one single, dextrous skip and jump.

When Jake had climbed the wall, he found himself in a back yard behind a decaying house whose windows were broken and whose frames were crumbling. Even in the darkness, he could see that the ground of the yard was littered with broken bricks and sticks. An old basketball hoop lay idly in a corner with a fractured drain pipe hanging limply from the wall above it. Empty, chewed up milk cartons rested among torn off twigs and branches underneath a hedge which had grown like tangled, unkempt hair into a sprawling mess.

In the centre of the yard stood an old, abandoned car, a dark blue BMW saloon whose tyres had been slashed and windows shattered. Its doors were ripped off and its once coveted upholstery had been torn to shreds. It rested on a bed of bricks like the carcass of a once great predator, its headlights staring like two lifeless eyes in the half light of the moon.

'We're here,' Christine whispered. Then she pulled on Jake's sleeve. 'This way.'

She led him beyond the BMW to another, smaller car, abandoned like the first, but concealed underneath the thick leaves and branches of an overhanging tree. Its bonnet was pointing into the front passenger door of the BMW. Its trunk was tight against the wall of the house.

'This is my home,' Christine said, pointing at the car beneath the tree.

Jake could see that it was a sports car. Although the wing mirror was hanging like a broken limb from its side, the windows of the car were still intact and its doors were also in place.

As Christine pulled on the handle, the door opened easily and Jake peered in. The front passenger seat, covered in a neatly folded sleeping bag and blue and red blankets, was set in full recline mode, its head rest covered in a pillowcase stuffed with feathers.

'I sleep this side,' Christine said, climbing into the car. 'You will have to sleep on the driver's side. If you move the seat right back as far as it will go you shouldn't be too uncomfortable, even with the steering column.'

'Thanks,' Jake replied, as he slid over the bonnet of the car and negotiated his way into the driver's seat, pulling on a lever underneath and forcing the disused runners into operation.

'This isn't too shabby,' he muttered.

'It's a 1964 Ford Consul Capri,' Christine said, 'one of the last of its kind. My father had one. He used to call it "old four eyes" because of its four headlights. I used to love going out for a drive with him. His had a white and black, mock leopard skin cover on the steering wheel, and he bought matching floor mats for the front footwells, too. The model he had even had a cigar lighter.'

'He sounds like a great dad,' Jake said.

'He was.'

Jake paused for a moment. 'I'd have loved to have had a daughter,' he said.

With that, the two began to bed themselves down for the night, Christine dragging worn blankets from behind her seat and offering them to Jake before she turned to her own routine.

'Don't worry, Jake. Gusto will be with us all night, keeping watch.'

Jake smiled.

'You'll have to bear with me,' she added. 'There's something I say out loud every night before I go to sleep. It's just a little prayer.'

'Are you religious?'

'No, I'm not!' Christine retorted. 'I'm not religious at all. But I am spiritual.'

'You're not the first person to say that to me,' Jake said.

Christine bowed her head and closed her eyes. 'Dear Heavenly Father, you tell us that you have a house and that in that house there are many rooms. I pray for all the people living on the streets, that you would find some rooms for them tonight. Amen.'

Jake whispered, 'Amen.'

———

That night Christine slept by Jake's side, her moonlit face endowed with a peace that made her look younger than she had in the coffee shop a few hours earlier.

Jake slept fitfully, trying to get his frame to meld with the contours of the driver's seat, moving from his back to his sides, bumping into the large steering wheel as he did.

Next morning, Jake awoke to the intermittent sound of birdsong. He stepped out of the car to stretch his aching muscles, observing both the weather-beaten Capri and its leafy garage. It was an extremely effective hiding place.

The house behind him had been gutted by fire. This home, which stood detached as well as deserted, had been visited by a disaster many years before and now lay forsaken like a stranded wreck on a lonely beach. The back yard had become the dumping ground for all manner of unwanted items. Beyond the protective arms of the overhanging tree, Jake saw a discarded fridge lying on its side next to a Belfast sink from a bygone era, its once white sides stained by mud and paint.

This is a rubbish tip, Jake thought, *but at least I should be safe here.*

As Jake shuffled around the Ford Capri, Christine awoke and rubbed her eyes. She called to him to come and have some breakfast, climbing out of the car as she did and moving to the trunk, which she opened. Delving into the boot, she lifted a shopping bag and brought it to the bonnet of the car, placing its contents on its rusty surface like a mother setting breakfast.

That morning, the two of them ate cheese and biscuits with some Coca Cola that had lost its fizz. They sat and talked for hours before napping in the warm October sun in the afternoon.

'We'll go out foraging tonight,' Christine said. 'Best to get a little sleep this afternoon. I'm out of supplies and we need to replenish the stocks.'

That night, well after midnight Jake guessed, they draped the car with the boughs of the overhanging tree before moving off together from their home into city streets, whose stony silences were broken from time to time by the sound of violent shouting and the wailing sirens of passing ambulances and police cars.

Christine, as streetwise as an urban fox, moved stealthily from neighbourhood to neighbourhood, her ears alert to the tiniest nuances of danger, her eyes darting from one shadowy outline to another, assessing its threat level with a refined instinct.

Two hours later, they returned to the car and deposited several bags of food and drinks they'd found into the boot, Christine rubbing her hands after manoeuvring the back door into place, adding that it was a good night's plunder and that Gusto was pleased with their haul. That night Christine said her little prayer again and the two companions, thrown together like flotsam and jetsam in an incoming tide, lay becalmed amid the rubble.

For the next two months life passed uneventfully, until the early hours of a mid-December morning, when their familiar nocturnal rhythm was disrupted while looting the bins behind an Italian restaurant.

Two homeless men had also targeted the premises, identifying the back yard as a promising source of alcohol. When they approached, Jake and Christine froze, thinking they had been discovered by waiters putting out the rubbish. When they saw that the men were vagrants, they relaxed and agreed to let them share the spoils.

Over the next half hour, their mutual pirating brought about an unanticipated solidarity. As the two men made to leave the yard, one of them asked if they could eat with them, adding that they would be glad of the company on a cold night like this. Christine, who had become a quick and discerning judge of character in her years of living rough, gauged that their intentions were harmless so agreed on hers and Jake's behalf.

About twenty minutes later, the four of them were huddled in the capacious porch of a Gothic church, sharing their plunder and their stories with each other.

'What's with you guys?' Jake asked.

One of the two men spoke up. 'We're both war veterans. We saw stuff in battle that's messed with our heads. I saw friends blown to pieces by improvised explosive devices. One of them was completely incinerated inside an armoured car when it ran into a roadside bomb. There was nothing left of him at all. My friend here was a sniper and saw through his scope the devastating effect of his weapon.'

'We are both trying to forget,' his friend said, drawing a grimy green bottle from the inside of his overcoat and lifting it to his stained lips.

After taking a large gulp, he thrust the bottle out towards Christine, who was crouching next to Jake in the dimly lit shelter.

'Have a swig,' he said to her. Jake noticed that his hand and arm were shaking.

'No thanks,' Christine replied.

The former soldier offered the bottle to Jake, who also refused it.

'It must be hard trying to forget,' Jake said, as the bottle returned to its owner.

'This helps,' the man replied.

He was about to continue when his friend put his finger to his lips. Christine had heard it too, the sound of a car parking on the road a few metres outside the entrance, beyond the cast iron gate that stood open in front of the church. As the four of them huddled in the shadows, they heard footsteps moving up the gravel path towards them. Without a sound, the two ex-soldiers leaped to their feet and moved swiftly to a position either side of the entrance. As they did, a tall man in a black top hat appeared, holding a torch in one hand and a pistol with a silencer in the other.

The Undertaker!

That single thought arrested Jake, causing his face to blanch with terror.

Is this how my life ends?

But Jake had not accounted for the veterans. They had said that there were things they could not forget. One of those things was their training. The moment they saw the gun, the two of them attacked the Undertaker in a pincer movement, one of them kickboxing the gun out of his hand with a deft and rapid action, the other standing on the weapon and immobilising the assailant in a strong arm lock.

'Who the hell do you think you are?' one of the veterans asked, looking up and down the man in the top hat and tails.

The Undertaker didn't answer.

'He's a murderer, that's what he is!' Jake said. 'He's after me because I owe him money from a poker game. He won't be satisfied until I'm dead.'

'Is that right?' the soldier said, standing menacingly in front of the Undertaker, whose face remained impassive. 'Well, I'm not afraid of you, you ugly sod. If you come back here again, you'll get a hiding.'

'He won't talk to you,' Jake said.

But Jake was wrong. As the Undertaker sneered at both of Jake's protectors, he reached his free hand out, pointing his long and gnarled finger towards Jake, who had now been joined by Christine.

'There must be blood,' the Undertaker said.

With that, he gazed into the eyes of the former soldier who had pinned his arm behind his back. The veteran, startled by the taller man's stare, loosened his grip and the Undertaker used his liberated right arm to brush himself down before turning with indifference to leave the scene. He marched beyond the iron gates and climbed inside the back of a chauffeur driven limousine.

'Good grief!' Jake stuttered, stumbling to his knees and then to the floor. 'That was close. Too close.'

'Yes, it was,' one of the men replied. 'We can't stay here,' he said. 'He'll be back, with others next time. We need to get rid of this gun and part company.'

They hurried out of the porch and made their way behind the church to the cemetery, where mossy grave stones protruded at an angle from the grassy turf. One of the men spotted a grave that had been freshly dug, no doubt waiting for a funeral the following day. A spade was lodged into the wet turf, blade first, next to it. He took the implement, jumped into the grave, and began to dig.

'Here, give me the gun,' he said to his mate, who passed it to him, holding the weapon by the silencer.

The impromptu gravedigger got to work and within two minutes had concealed the hit man's weapon under the clay at the bottom of the grave.

'Didn't think I'd ever dig another trench in my life,' he said. He offered a hand to help his mate from the hole.

'We'd better go our separate ways,' the digger said.

Christine nodded.

'Let's get out of here,' she said to Jake.

An hour later, they were back inside the Ford Capri, Jake holding onto the oversized steering wheel as he trembled with the aftershock.

'Look,' he said. 'I think we should split up, too. I'm too dangerous. Those I get close to end up dead. I'm not good for you.'

'That's not your decision,' Christine replied. 'Listen, Jake. I've been on the streets for nearly ten years, missing my dad like crazy. You come walking into my world one night and pass on a message from him, for which I'm more grateful than I can say. If I stay with you, that's my choice. At the end of the day, the only thing that ever brightens up our lives is a little bit of love. Well, I've found a little bit of love from you – some of my father's love. And I choose love.'

Jake took his hands from the steering wheel and turned towards Christine, stretching them out towards her, taking her hands in his.

'Are you sure?' he asked.

'Absolutely,' she replied. 'I choose love.'

'Okay,' Jake said. 'Say your little prayer and then let's sleep.'

And she did.

The next morning, Jake and Christine woke to find that the yard beyond their sheltered home was dusted with snow.

'I'm dreaming of a white Christmas,' Christine sang.

'It's magical,' Jake said.

'It's also lethal,' Christine added, 'at least if you're without blankets and a shelter.'

'I know,' Jake said. 'Nearly a year ago I would have died had it not been for the intervention of a German Shepherd.'

'They're lovely dogs,' Christine mused. 'We used to have one when I was little. They'd do anything to protect you and they're incredibly loyal to you if you're sleeping rough. They're the best street angels, Alsatians and Labradors.'

Later that day, as darkness fell, the two friends left the yard. Christine had suggested that they search for items that could form the basis of a Christmas dinner. Jake loved the idea, so the two of them set out towards a retail park just outside the city limits where brand new outlet stores and supermarkets competed for people's cash and custom. Christine had been there once before and brought the crowbar from the boot of her car. The walk had taken over four hours, but her exertions had been rewarded by an unprecedented haul of meat and drink, sweets and sandwiches.

By the time the two of them arrived at the floodlit parking lots, the snow was falling, causing cars to slip and spin. Christine pointed to a superstore on their left and the two of them scampered between cars and shrubs, trees and trolley parks, until they were behind the store.

Jake tried to open one of the large bins in the yard. 'It's got a padlock,' he cried.

'No problem,' Christine said, drawing the metal bar from her Wermacht greatcoat.

'I found it in the trunk of the Capri a few years ago,' she whispered.

With that she took the jack in her hands and crowbarred the lock until it snapped. On opening the lid, they found a cornucopia of rejected food and drinks.

'This is a heavenly haul,' Christine said.

First into their bags was an ample-breasted chicken, fully cooked, its skin a golden brown. It was still entombed within its packet and only a day past its sell-by date.

'That'll do for our turkey,' Christine said.

Next into the bag was a large, sealed tub of potato salad, 'Instead of roast potatoes,' Christine remarked, followed by an unsold pack of Indian delicacies – mostly samosas and bhajis – 'Our vegetables,' Jake suggested.

For dessert, they found a huge transparent tub of custard trifle loitering beneath a stash of smoky bacon crisps. With the addition of three sealed packets of fine cheese, and several cans of Coca Cola, their bounty was complete.

'We can't take any more than this,' Christine said. 'We need to leave some for others.'

The two darted off with a shopping bag each and bolted through the crowded car park. The snow was cascading now and the slush beneath their feet had made its way inside Jake's trainers.

At about three o'clock in the morning they climbed over the wall into their yard, their bags held tight by frozen hands and fingers. A few seconds later, they had fallen into the front seats of the hidden car and were rubbing their hands warm again.

Before the sun rose, the two of them tucked into Christmas dinner al Fresco in a Ford Capri, high-fiving each other with childlike joy with every course, toasting their friendship.

By five o'clock their stomachs were full and their hearts were glad, so glad, in fact, that both began to sing.

Jingle bells, jingle bells
Jingle all the way
Oh, what fun it is to ride
In a one horse open sleigh.

It was not long after their carolling that Christine and Jake were fast asleep, breathing deeply and with contentment as the sun rose and then began to dim again.

When the two awoke, the snow was plummeting and both of them felt the cold.

'We'd better get to the cafe again for a hot drink,' Christine suggested, wiping her eyes.

'I agree,' said Jake.

'Come on, Gusto,' Christine said.

They left the yard, forcing their aching joints into hurried action. Within an hour, they had arrived at the cafe and were sitting by a steamy window, cradling mugs of hot chocolate and reminiscing about their Christmas dinner.

'That was a happy night,' Jake said. 'I think we can definitely say that we did that with gusto.'

They laughed as they sipped their drinks, enjoying the afterglow of both their beverages and memories. They hummed as carols played, Christine breaking into quiet singing as the old speakers crackled.

O ye beneath life's crushing load,
Whose forms are bending low,
Who toil along the climbing way
With painful steps and slow;
Look now, for glad and golden hours
Come swiftly on the wing;
Oh rest beside the weary road
And hear the angels sing.

Christine returned to humming but Jake, who had been struck by the beauty of her voice, interrupted her.

'Do you believe in angels?' he asked.

'Yes, I do. But I think they visit us in disguise as passing strangers, helpers, comforters – rarely in white with massive wings.'

Jake turned to his right and cleared some of the steam from the cafe window next to him, pressing his face against the pane.

He leaned back towards the table and then forward towards Christine, staring for a moment into her languid eyes.

'You know,' he said, 'it has surprised me how many people living rough think like you.'

'What do you mean?'

'Well, if I'm honest, I've met more people who believe in God in the last twelve months than I had in the previous twelve years put together.'

'That's because the kingdom of heaven is for the desperate.'

By now their mugs were empty and a line of people needing seats was building up.

'It's time,' Christine said.

They stood up and buttoned up their coats, wrapping their scarves around their necks, replacing their woollen hats on their heads and pulling their gloves tight around their hands and fingers. As they left the cafe, Jake pushed both his hands into the pockets of his overcoat and felt the shape of a small packet in the lining on the left-hand side.

'Oh, wow!' he exclaimed. 'I'd completely forgotten about these.'

'Forgotten about what?'

'I've been holding on to these for a long, long time,' he answered, withdrawing a tiny packet wrapped within creased and faded Christmas paper from his pocket. 'They're for my boys. I bought them two years ago for their Christmas presents. They are designer watches with their favourite superheroes printed on them.'

Jake placed the box in the palm of his hand and stared at it. 'I have never been able to give this to my son.'

'I'm sure you will one day,' Christine remarked. 'You have a father's heart. Maybe you should go home, Jake. Maybe it's time.'

Jake closed his hand around the box and took a step into

the icy road. Christine was holding onto Jake and looking up into his face. Neither of them saw the limousine lurking like a stalking jaguar further down the road. It had been enshrouded in the late afternoon gloom and its two occupants had been lying in wait.

As Jake and Christine left the cafe, the car pulled into the road and began to accelerate.

As it did, Jake's feet slid upon some ice, sending his arms into a spin and his tiny package into the night air.

'No!' he cried, as the package fell into the path of the car.

Jake let go of Christine's hand and fell forwards into the road, landing on his knees, his hands groping in the slush.

'No, Jake!' Christine screamed.

Just as Jake's flailing fingers touched the box, he saw the oncoming car to his right.

He turned, panic rising in his stomach.

The sound of the vehicle grew stronger and closer, like a wave about to break.

Jake's eyes were now staring into the car's front lights, both on full beam.

He froze. But just as he did so, he felt a violent push at his back which forced him forward into the middle of the road, causing him to slide away from the onrushing limo.

He turned to see what had hit him.

It was Christine.

The inky bonnet of the car hit her broadside, sending her frail body into the air as if she was a flimsy doll.

She landed with a thud on the pavement as the car hurried away into the darkness.

Jake groaned. 'No, Jesus, no!'

She lay still upon the snowy sidewalk, her face turned up

towards the stars.

'Christine!' Jake shouted. 'Christine!'

Jake stumbled as fast as he could over the ice towards her crumpled body. He knelt beside her, his arms reaching towards her, pulling her head into his lap, weeping as he cradled her.

A woman passing by shouted, 'That was a hearse!'

A man who could have been her husband added, 'I've got the number!'

Jake shouted to them, 'Call an ambulance. Please, call an ambulance.'

He turned back to Christine. There was blood, almost black in colour, working its way down from her nose to her lips. Her eyes flickered momentarily as it entered her mouth.

Christine whispered.

'He said… he said… there must… be blood.'

'No, Christine!' Jake cried.

'Yes,' Christine replied. 'Mine… will have to do.'

'It was supposed to be mine,' he cried.

Christine continued to look up. 'I want… I want… to go home… home,' she said.

She coughed hard and a spatter of blood fell upon the snow.

'I want… to see… my dad… again. Promise me, promise me… take Gusto… wherever you go. Promise?'

Jake looked down into Christine's eyes.

'Oh, Christine,' he sobbed. 'Why did you do this?'

'Because love… love is a choice,' she said.

With that, her final breath rose and mingled with the wind.

Jake looked up, his eyes waterlogged with tears. People were milling all around him, some from the cafe that he and Christine had just left. They were leaning over him, speaking about what they had and hadn't seen.

As Jake looked at the road, he saw a diminutive package torn and crushed into the wet ice that covered the tarmac. His son's gift watch was now protruding from its wet wrapping, its glass broken, its hands stuck forever at 6 p.m.

Jake lowered Christine's head to the ground, using his scarf as a pillow. He could hear the first sounds of a siren in the distance.

He bowed down and kissed the forehead of his friend, his tears falling onto her face as he gently closed her eyes.

He whispered into her ears, 'Dear Heavenly Father, please find a room in your house for Christine tonight.'

He stood up, taking one last look at Christine. Then he turned to his right in the direction in which the black limo had accelerated.

He walked at first, maintaining his balance as best he could. Then, as the ice turned to snow, he began to jog.

Finally, he broke into a run.

He wanted blood.

The Undertaker's blood.

Hey Dad

It's Christmas again so I thought I would write you another letter
Mummy has found an Xbox game for me as my main present
Its second hand but she says it will play like new – the shop promised
It's a war game and I'm going to get to shoot with a proper machine gun
Its really really cool
I love it
You'd love it too
I moved to my new school in September
I wear a uniform
It's a black blazer with the school badge on it
I wear Bobby's grey trousers – the ones he wore when he was in year 7 too
He's getting tall, just like you
No one picks a fight with him cos he's SOOOO big!
Its nice having a big brother looking out for me
Its a kind of like having you around
Though not the same
I'm getting good at sport
I did well on sports day in my old school
I won two prizes
And I play in goal for my year in football
Mr Phillips says I could go far if I train hard
Hes been cheering me on and that makes me feel good
Id like to play for Chelsea
I have a Chelsea football shirt which I wear after school

I watch their matches at a friend's house – they have the sports channels on their TV

I still have your coat

Its hanging on the back of my bedroom door, under my dressing gown

And your shoes are under my bed

Where my secret shoe box is

That's where I keep my letters to you

Under your favrite shoes

In the secret shoe box

Not even mummy knows its there

Only you do now

I wish Mum was happy

Uncle Pete doesn't come round

I don't think he likes Mum anymore

Mum is now sad a lot

She said the other day she thought you might be dead

No one has heard from you, no one knows where you are – not even the police

Then she got mad with herself and said she was cross cos she had forgot to trust God to keep you safe

I have asked God to send some angels to watch over you and guide you home

I hope they are working hard

I made a poster for you

Mummy sent it round the country – we are hoping that you see it

I had a dream last night I saw the sea – it was very dark and very ruff

You were in a sailing ship – like on the old movies

It looked like a pirate's ship
A storm made it sink and you were in the sea, holding on to
a broken bit of mast
You saw a light shining on and off and swam to it
When you got there it was land and the light was coming
from my bedroom window
Our home had turned into a light house – which I thought
was kind of cool
I woke up excited cos even though you might be in truble, I
was happy that you were alive
Cos some days I get very sad that you might not be
I was also happy cos you found your way home
Please come home soon
I still love you dad
I'm not giving up on you xxx

4. The Trucker

Jake pursued the dark shape of the limo as the snow poured onto the gritted roads. Only when the car stopped at traffic lights did he think there was any chance of catching it, but then it accelerated away into the murky night, like a sleek and prized shark evading its hunter.

Jake slowed down. His hands were numb and his feet were now beginning to shuffle more than run. As fatigue rose like hemlock from his legs, he wished he had returned to the Ford Capri to hide beneath a mound of sleeping bags and blankets for the night. Except that he could not face the car without Christine.

'This is useless,' he muttered under the moaning wind. 'I'm so sorry, Christine.'

Jake now took stock of where he was. He was standing in the main street of the city, with department stores, designer shops, sandwich bars and fast food restaurants on both sides of a road where cars and buses jostled. He trudged past a theatre designed like an ancient temple with six giant Corinthian columns resting on colossal, moulded plinths. A church rose above him, its tower and leaning buttresses illuminated in the gloom. As he limped past, he looked up and saw a gargoyle protruding from the church's wall, its clawed feet clinging to the ancient stone and its grotesque, demon face locked in a scornful grin. Wiping some snow from his eyes, he noticed that a small jet of water had frozen as it passed through the creature's gawping mouth. It was now hanging like a stalactite above the pavement, just above his head.

Jake decided not to the try the church's heavy doors and walked on along the snowy sidewalk. As he sloped past the statue of a city benefactor, his eyes were drawn to a flashing neon sign.

'Welcome to the Father's House.'

A few moments later he was studying the words on a sign board just in front of a recently refurbished building.

'Homeless Mission. City Tabernacle.'

Jake stumbled up the frozen steps and through a glass-panelled door, walking into a foyer where a young woman with short, pixie styled hair stood behind a brand new pinewood counter.

'Welcome, stranger,' she said. 'Do you need help?'

'I need shelter.'

'Are you homeless?'

Jake grunted. It took him several seconds to answer.

'Since Christmas Day last year.'

'Well, you are welcome. This is the Father's house. We have many rooms. I'm sure I can find one for you.'

Jake grunted again.

'Why don't you take the weight off your feet? There are some chairs in a side room just over there,' she said, pointing to a corridor leading off the foyer. 'I'll bring a coffee and a form for us to fill in. Do you take milk and sugar?'

Jake nodded.

The woman closed the counter and walked through a freshly painted, bright white door into a newly fitted kitchenette. As Jake ambled to the side room, he could hear the satisfying sound of a kettle being switched on and water beginning to boil. A moment later, he was in a sitting room. Spying a tartan armchair broader than the rest, he lowered himself into its deeply padded seat, savouring the welcome of its cushions and placing his weary hands upon its curved and scrolling arm rests.

He scanned the room. All over the walls there were cork-backed notice boards with posters pinned on every available space. Each board was covered in the photographs of people missing on the streets, many of them teenagers, with messages from loved ones printed on them.

'Have you seen this man?'

'This is my daughter.'

'Jimmy, this is your mum. I love you.'

'Leanne, please – please – contact us.'

'Mike, I beg you, tell us you're okay.'

Jake stood to his feet. There was a wooden table with a white cloth opposite him, covered in unlit tealights, with a box of matches and two white tapirs lying on a smaller table next to it.

A crumpled yellow card contained an exhortation for visitors to light a candle for a missing loved one and to say a prayer for their homecoming.

A solitary scented candle, much taller and thicker than the tealights, was flickering on a wooden shelf just above the table. It had a white, laminated card with some words printed in an antique font.

'The fire must be kept burning continuously on the altar, day and night.' Leviticus 6.13.

Jake's heart began to race.

He turned to a wall that seemed to burst with photographs, black and white and colour, too.

And then he saw it.

In the centre was his own photograph, at the top of a piece of A4 paper that had been lodged into the cork by a blood-red pin. He was wearing a suit and tie. His hair was cut short and his face was clean shaven.

'THIS IS MY DADDY', it read at the top. Underneath, 'I love my dad and I miss him. If you see him, please ask him to come home.'

Jake's eyes began to fill as they lowered to the end of the photocopied, hand-written inscription.

'From Tommy.'

He fell to his knees.

Jake's heart melted like the snow on his soles. He was desperate now, utterly desperate, to see his family. It was as if for two years he had slipped into a parallel universe, into an alternate reality, and now he saw the stark futility and hopelessness of all his wanderings. He would not be a fugitive any more. He would return and tell his family that he was deeply sorry. He would make it up to them for the rest of his life. It was time, he decided, to go home.

Jake stumbled to his feet and bolted as fast as his weakened legs would carry him from the room, slamming the door as he left.

He brushed past the young woman with his coffee on his way out, murmuring a garbled 'sorry' as he fled from the building.

'Sorry!' he repeated, shouting it as loud as he could as he bounded through the door and onto the streets.

He ran from the city centre, pushing through unyielding shoppers, shoulder-barging several people in his headlong dash, their shopping bags spilling some of their contents onto the freezing sidewalk. He had to get to the southbound motorway.

Jake ran until his lungs were sore and his legs began to buckle. He was flagging now.

He figured he had run for at least two hours, but he could not be sure.

'Where am I?' he said between shallow breaths and violent shivers.

Jake was now finding it harder and harder to stay on his feet. His sense of direction was gone, and so was his ability to reason. In one wild and manic moment, Jake removed his overcoat, thinking he was overheating, and tossed it over a wall into the night, never to see it, or the Christmas present within it, again.

He was on the edge – on the edge of the city and on the edge of sanity.

A few hundred metres ahead of him, Jake saw a house beside the main road. He could just make out the words 'Roadside Cafe' on a floodlit board. The windows were lit up by festive lights, each light a wooden bridge standing above a carved stable, and supporting seven imitation candles with holly and ivy at their base.

'If I can make it there, I'll be okay,' Jake mumbled.

But he had no more strength to walk. His energy was sapped from several hours of marching through the heavy snow. He was no longer even shivering.

Suddenly, Jake heard feet crunching behind him, both on his right and left. He turned to see two women reaching out towards his arms, bearing each of his beneath their own.

'Come on, pet,' one of them said. 'You look all done in. Let's get you to the cafe. You'll be warm in there and Ma Ruby's hot chocolate is to die for.'

With that, his escorts, adorned in Santa hats with trailing bobbles, took the strain and started to walk Jake forwards. They made it to the hedge adjacent to the house.

'Good luck and a happy Christmas,' they said.

Jake stood and watched them strutting down the street. Their winter coats reached down to just below their thighs, revealing short, red Christmas dresses, black diamond net tights and shiny calf-length boots.

He smiled and turned towards the entrance of the cafe, but as he did, he slipped on a tiny patch of untreated ice just beneath the stone steps leading to the door. He careered forwards in a sudden dive, his floundering hands trying to find some purchase on a low brick wall. But it was to no avail. With a thud, Jake's face hit the base of the steps. His mouth and lips went numb.

'That's all I needed,' he gasped.

He rose, his head spinning. As he looked down at the steps, he noticed that tiny red dots were forming in the ground. He wiped his hand across his face. As he did, the tips of his blue and purple fingers turned a bright and vivid red. His stomach churned as he saw fragments one of his teeth stick for a moment to a fingernail.

He staggered up the steps to the entrance, pushed open the door with his elbow, limped into the room and fell, accompanied by the clatter of a tumbling wooden chair.

Jake composed himself and looked at his surroundings. He was in a room with six pinewood tables, four 1950s American diner chairs standing at each. The walls were painted fresh peach, the ceiling in warm white. On his left, against the wall, a cast iron wood burner with a glass window was glowing. A strong fire was roaring away inside and a black flue pipe was taking its smoke up the wall, through the roof of the house into the night air outside.

A flat screen television hanging in one corner was set on a news channel with subtitles, without sound.

Ahead of him, at the far end of the room, stood a wooden counter, also painted a fresh peach colour, with the words 'Ma Ruby's Roadside Cafe' painted in strident red capitals on a stretch of white wall behind and above it.

On the counter stood a small, imitation Christmas tree with flashing lights, next to a vintage, Coca Cola branded cash register with press down keys, like those on a flute.

Beyond the counter, in a recess, packets of repair tools and engine accessories were hanging on the walls above a double bowled aluminium kitchen sink with a single, overhanging tap.

Jake, aware that four truckers were now staring at him, tried to get to his feet. At that moment, a woman appeared from a kitchen behind the counter. She was in a pink and white striped apron and was now pouring tea into several mugs from a jaded china teapot with a woollen cosy. She had striking blond hair in a 1960s flip style, and bright blue eyes, now filled with indignation. The moment Jake looked at her, he saw the word *mother*.

'Is someone going to help him, then?' she asked.

A black-skinned man, sitting on his own in an alcove, stopped humming a song playing on a multicoloured jukebox and began to make his way towards Jake.

He leaned down and with a huge hand lifted him effortlessly. Noticing the blood, he took a table napkin and pressed it carefully to Jake's bearded face.

'My name is Matt,' he said, removing the napkin and stretching out his hand.

Jakes looked at him. He tried to use his gift, but the man seemed unreadable.

Jake paused for a moment, wondering if he could trust him. Then his desperation trumped his caution.

'I'm Jake.'

Jake took hold of Matt's hand.

'Let me get you something to warm you up,' Matt whispered.

Before Jake even had the opportunity to answer, Matt had turned towards the counter and put in an order. 'One of your Christmas dinners please, Ma Ruby, and a hot mug of your best builder's tea.'

'Coming right up, my darling.'

Matt sat down at a table covered in a chequered cloth, bidding Jake to sit down too. Jake put his head in his hands, covering his mouth with his fingers, wiping the blood from his tooth, groaning under the cover of the festive melodies.

A minute later, Ma Ruby brought the biggest mug of tea that Jake had ever seen. He drank it, savouring every mouthful, until only a thin layer of sugar lay like treacle at the bottom.

Next came the Christmas dinner – generous slices of turkey accompanied by carrots and peas, stuffing and roast potatoes, covered by dark brown gravy and lashings of bread sauce.

Jake tucked in, mumbling the word 'thanks' while navigating his food around the sore remains of his broken tooth.

When he had eaten every morsel, he looked up. There were red, green and golden ribbons hanging from the ceiling, along with a brown banner saying MERRY CHRISTMAS. A wreath with artificial cones and bright red berries was fixed to a door leading to the toilets and a sprig of plastic mistletoe was hanging above Ma Ruby's counter. In a far corner stood an eight-foot Christmas tree sporting an extravagant array of stars, baubles, love hearts, and golden fairies, illuminated by lights of countless different colours, all carefully guarded by a white winged angel with a golden halo attached to the top of the tree.

Jake relaxed. A smell of rich gravy and apricot stuffing filled the air and he could still taste the cranberry jelly on his tongue. He listened to Frank Sinatra and Bing Cosby on the jukebox singing 'Silent Night'. As he did so, a scene began to play out in Jake's memory, of a time when he and his wife Sally put up the decorations for the very first Christmas that their first son, Billy, was old enough to enjoy. He remembered putting up the nativity set on a table beneath the main window in their living room. It was unusual in that every part of it was made of knitted wool. It was also very old and had been in his family for many years. One or two of the characters were beginning to look their age and had become decidedly frayed and discoloured.

Jake remembered taking Joseph out of the nativity scene and saying to Sally, 'He's looking the worse for wear. It won't notice if he's missing this Christmas. Let's take him out and make a new one. If I remember right, he's really rather redundant anyway in the original story.'

Jake shuddered as he recalled the indignant reaction of his wife, who simply seized the figure from his hands and placed him back beside the crib.

'Better a worn-out father than no father at all,' she had said.

The sound of animated conversation from the four men at their table snapped him out of his daydream.

'What's with those guys?' he asked Matt.

'They're truckers,' Matt replied. 'Don't mind them. People who drive for the same firm often sit together, but they're friendly enough. There's good camaraderie between pretty well all truckers, especially over the radio.'

'What about you?' Jake asked. 'What do you do?'

'I'm a trucker too,' Matt answered. 'Articulated lorries. Mine's just outside in the lay-by. It's the one with the red cab at the front.'

'Do you enjoy it?'

'Man, I love it. The only thing I don't like is spending a lot of time away from my family. But they're very supportive and in any case, I'm in touch with them all the time wherever I go.'

'Where are you heading?' Jake enquired.

'I've been here dropping off my cargo and I'm now on my way back down south, though in this blizzard it may take a while.'

Matt paused for a moment before continuing. 'Listen, I am supposed to drive for another four hours until I have to sleep in the cab tonight. I was thinking, I could do with some company. Do you need a lift?'

Jake took a closer look at Matt. Standing at about six-foot-six inches high, he was enormous. Not only was he tall, he also had the widest, thickest neck that Jake had ever seen. He was a colossus of a man, but he seemed genuine and kind.

'If you have room,' he said.

'There's room,' Matt said. 'Do you have any belongings?'

'No, I've lost everything. And now I've got this to add to my troubles.' Jake pointed to his mouth.

Matt looked for a moment at Jake's lower lip, now swollen and stained with clotted blood.

'You mind if I look at that?'

'Why – are you a dentist?'

'No,' Matt chuckled. 'But I can help.'

Jake nodded.

Matt peered inside his open mouth and touched the tip of the broken, bruised incisor in his lower jaw. Jake braced himself, expecting pain, but felt nothing – nothing, that is, except a strange anaesthetising warmth.

Matt sensed Jake's caution.

'Don't be nervous. I have a gift. It runs in my family. My father has it.'

Jake felt heat flow through his tooth and gums and with it, a peace he had never felt before.

Matt withdrew his finger.

Jake manoeuvred his tongue to feel the broken tooth with its tip. His broken tooth was whole again.

And the pain had gone.

'How?… How?' Jake stammered.

'It's in the family,' Matt said. 'All his life my father has prayed for the sick. People travel from miles around to the healing services he conducts. Many times, as a boy, I remember walking into the sanctuary and seeing people on stretchers. I saw my father hold these broken people in his arms, weep over them, whisper a prayer in their ear, and then move on.'

Matt sipped his tea and smiled.

'As I grew older, he would take me with him round the rows and rows of desperate people and we would see wonderful things. Soon I found that my father's gift was my gift, too, and we have never stopped believing, and we've never stopped praying for those who have a need, whether they go to church or not.'

Jake scratched his head.

'Do people ever think you're a bit – well – weird?'

Matt roared with laughter. 'Oh yes, of course. Some of my fellow truckers do.'

Matt looked round at the four truckers, who were whispering. He raised his voice so they could hear.

'They tend to ask my help when they're in need but frown when they're not.'

With that, Matt stood to his feet and pushed his chair underneath the table.

'Let's go,' he said.

The two walked towards the door, thanked Ma Ruby for her hospitality, and walked outside as Bing Crosby sang 'Have Yourself a Merry Little Christmas' on the jukebox.

Once outdoors, Matt took Jake by the arm and led him past several trucks to where his own was parked. Jake could not see much in the darkness but he was aware of a big red cab looming large in front of him. As Matt approached his vehicle, he flipped a switch on his key and the cab lit up.

'Oh my,' Jake exclaimed as a myriad of bright white bulbs suddenly erupted into light, revealing a Coca Cola logo on the front. 'You drive one of the Christmas Coca Cola trucks!'

'Yes, sir,' Matt replied.

'I have always loved these.'

'There's a lot to love about them,' Matt said. 'Do you know how many light bulbs there are on this truck?'

'Hundreds.'

'Thousands, more like. 3,200 to be precise, all pouring light onto the painting of the Coca Cola Santa on the sides, toasting passing drivers with his bottle of trademark soda.'

Matt chuckled. 'What would Christmas be without the Coca Cola trucks?' he concluded.

He walked around the truck, unlocked the driver's door, climbed in and reached for the passenger door to open it.

'Here, let me give you a hand,' he shouted to Jake. 'It's a bit of a leap when you're not used to it. Put your foot on the ledge just above the wheel and I'll do the rest.'

As Matt reached past him to close the door, Jake noticed a tattooed name, one letter on each of the trucker's five knuckles.

'Who's Jenny?' he asked.

'My wife. We've been married for fifteen years and have two daughters, Melissa and Jemma. They're my life.'

Matt pulled up the sleeve of his tartan, cotton shirt and revealed a tattoo on his left forearm. It had a finely drawn picture of a rich red love heart with the word 'Daddy' at the top, and the names of his two daughters beneath.

'See, they're always on the road with me, even when they're still at home.'

Jake noticed sprigs of holly taped to the top of the cab, just beneath the windshield. There were Christmas decorations everywhere – a miniature Christmas tree, a few crackers, several stickers with a snowman and some children, and a fake robin. In addition, there was a photograph held by chewing gum to the dashboard showing a young mum playing happily with two laughing, giddy daughters with burgeoning Afro hairstyles, skipping in the back yard of a modest home.

Before Jake could ask any more questions, the engine thundered into life.

'Let's be getting you home now,' Matt said as the headlights blazed in front of the cab.

A Christmas carol immediately began to pour out of the speakers.

'You'll have to excuse the music,' Matt shouted above the noise. 'This time of year, I listen to carols. Every Christmas, Jenny and the girls give me a new album. I'm a bit of a festive fanatic, or at least that's what Jenny says.'

Jake smiled.

Within minutes, Matt was belting out the carols as if there was no tomorrow. Jake had to admit, the man could sing. He sang with a commanding resonance and he sang with conviction, as if he truly believed every word.

Over the next few minutes, as the Coca Cola truck pulled out of the lorry park and onto the south bound freeway, 'O Little

Town of Bethlehem' blended into 'Once in Royal David's City', and then into 'O Come All Ye Faithful'.

As Matt sang with his rich baritone voice, even Jake began to hum along to old familiar tunes and words.

The holly bears a berry
As red as any blood
And Mary bore sweet Jesus Christ
To do poor sinners good
O the rising of the sun
And the running of the deer
The playing of the merry organ
Sweet singing of the choir.

Jake sank back into the passenger's seat and leaned his head against the window. He stared at the metronomic movements of the wipers and watched as the snow fell on the window between the chasing blades.

I've made such a mess of my life, he thought.

Matt stopped singing and turned the music down.

'I know what you're thinking.'

'What?'

'Sometimes I see things sort of unexpectedly. They come out of nowhere. Usually they are like a dream sequence, or a picture, or a series of scenes.'

'Are you clairvoyant?' Jake asked.

'I wouldn't use that word myself,' Matt replied. 'My mother was a seer. She could see things that others couldn't. She was given visions often when she least expected it.'

'What did you see?' Jake asked.

'I saw a young woman in a shawl of white feathers standing between two boys, one aged about fourteen, the other about eight. This person, she looked like an angel, wanted you to know that the boys are safe. Does that mean anything to you?'

Jake's heart was racing.

'Yes. I have two sons, Billy and Tommy. They'd be about those ages by now. I was, well, I was kind of thinking about them again just then. And I was wondering to myself if there was anyone looking out for my boys in the same way that you look out for your girls.'

'It seems like there's an angel on their shoulders,' Matt said.

As a carol ended, Matt slowed the engine until the truck was moving at no more than twenty miles an hour.

'What happened to you, my friend?'

As Matt continued to drive slowly through the blizzard, Jake told his story. He told him about the rage that had grown about what he had missed in his life, how he had begun to seek excitement in gambling, how he'd grown to resent his wife for reading his true motives, and how he had walked out on his family on Christmas Eve, driving north to Casino City. He described the intoxicating joyride playing poker, his time in the hotel and his relationship with Sandra. He told Matt everything and all the while Matt kept quiet.

When Jake had finished his tale, Matt reached forward to the computer monitor and pressed a few touch sensitive buttons.

'I want you to listen to this,' he said.

As Jake rested back in his seat, he heard the first bars of a piano tune. It sounded like something from an old Western movie and had a cadence that was instantly familiar. When he heard the first word of the song, he recognised it. It was his favourite hit as a teenager, and he had even sung it once to Sally in a karaoke bar when they were in their early twenties, before love's springtime had ended.

Desperado, why don't you come to your senses...

'This isn't a carol,' Jake muttered.
'Just listen, Jake.'

Don't you draw the Queen of Diamonds, boy,
She'll beat you if she's able.
You know the Queen of Hearts is always your best bet.

As the piano continued to play and the singer continued to sing, Jake felt the sting of a tear forming in his right eye.

Desperado, oh you ain't getting no younger
Your pain and your hunger
They're driving you home

The tears were streaming from both Jake's eyes now.

Your prison is walking through this world all alone.

Jake put his head in his hands.

Don't your feet get cold in the winter time?

Matt turned the volume up to drown the sound of Jake's gasping.

You better let somebody love you, before it's too late.

As the piano slowed and the tune reached its quiet conclusion, Jake's sobs subsided.
'I'm desperate,' he said.
Matt reached out his big hand and touched Jake's shoulder. 'We all get desperate sometimes.'

'I've never been this desperate.'

Matt grasped Jake's shoulder. 'Someone once said that the kingdom of heaven is for the desperate,' he said.

Jake jolted. 'That's what Christine once told me.'

'Well, she was right.'

'She was always right.'

Matt smiled.

'So you believe in right and wrong, Jake?'

'I used to, but somewhere along the way I lost my true north.'

Matt pointed in front of him. 'Look at this tachometer. It measures the number of revolutions per minute. All trucks like this are kitted out with one. This one here has details of this vehicle's name, registration, and times. As soon as I start driving, the tacho starts to work. If I fail to switch it on or if I break it, I'm liable to a huge fine and get points on my license. It measures the time I drive and the speed I go. If I drive too many hours, I might get tired and cause an accident. If I go too fast, I might plough into a car with a family in.'

Jake remembered Christine's pulverised body and shuddered.

'This instrument keeps me driving within reasonable time limits, and within sensible speeds. It's a constant reminder to me that I have to give an account of my speed and my hours.'

Jake nodded. 'Every vehicle should have one,' he said.

'And every human being, too.'

'What do you mean?'

'This tacho is like our conscience, and our conscience is our inbuilt guide designed to help us live within safe limits.'

'That's my problem, then,' Jake said. 'I ripped out my tachometer on Christmas Eve two years ago. Ever since then I've been driving too fast and too far and I've devastated my family in the process.'

Jake had his head in his hands again. 'My life is just one almighty car crash.'

Matt pulled into a lay-by and stopped the truck.

As the engine grew silent, Jake whispered, 'What have I done?'

Matt reached patted Jake's shoulder.

'The important question now,' he said, 'is not just what have you done, it's what do you do?'

'So, what do I do?'

'Only you can answer that, my friend.'

Jake looked out of the large front windows of the cab into the darkness. He thought of Sally and remembered the good times they had shared in their courtship and during the early years of their marriage. He remembered the births of his children and the intense joy he had felt at being a father. He remembered their first baths and the loud splashing of water and bubbles, and the sound of squealing and laughter. He remembered the first word Billy had ever uttered, 'Dada', and Tommy's first hug. He remembered dinner dates and children's parties, walks in the woods and picnics on the beach. He remembered buying uniforms and first days at school. And as he did, a great sadness began to seize his heart. He knew he had been selfish. He knew that Sally and the boys had not deserved his desertion. He knew he had allowed his own wounded history to repeat itself and that he had no one to blame except himself. And he knew above all – with an ache that transcended every other ache that had ever gnawed at his soul – that he wanted to go home.

'Father in heaven,' he whispered. 'Show me the way home.'

After several minutes, Matt started up the engine, pulled out onto the road, and spoke again.

'Jake, you mentioned going home. Have you thought this through?'

'No, I haven't.'

'Man, you can't just show up without warning your family.'

'I know.'

'You need to tell your wife and kids. You need to give them time to prepare themselves. Put yourself in their position.'

'How can I warn them?' Jake asked.

'You can phone them. Borrow my mobile and let them know you're on your way.'

'What do I say?'

'Just a few words.'

Matt pulled the handset from his pocket as he kept one hand on the wheel. Jake took the phone and cradled it in both hands. In his mind, he tried to compose a short message, but it felt impossible to reduce all his sorrows and hopes into a few simple sentences. In the end, he touched the keyboard with his trembling fingers, pressing down the keys to phone a number he hadn't used for two years. He made the connection and put the trembling handset to his ear.

Jake heard the phone ringing and tried to compose himself.

The tone carried on for what seemed like an eternity and he was all set to give up when suddenly it stopped, and he heard his wife's voice for the first time since he had left.

For a moment, he wanted to interrupt and tell her that he loved her, but then he realised that Sally wasn't there, that what he was hearing was the sound of a message on her voicemail.

'We're not able to come to the phone right now, but if you leave a message after the tone, the children and I will get back to you.'

Jake breathed a deep sigh of relief. She had said, 'the children and I'. There had been no mention of a new man in her life.

He composed himself and then began.

'Sally, boys, it's me. It's Daddy. I don't know if you're there... at home... but it's me. I want to say sorry... I'm so, so sorry. I'm going to be passing by tomorrow night. I just want to say hello. I won't blame you at all if you feel that's not a good idea. I know I've really blown it and I just wanted to come home for a moment and… and… I just want to see you again. I've messed up so badly, I know that, but please… please… please would you consider… if you thought it possible…'

Jake did not get to finish his sentence. The line cut out as the message box filled.

'I did it,' Jake said.

'You did it, man.'

'I wouldn't blame them if they decided to be out, or to leave a message on the door saying 'go away'. They'd have every right to do that.'

'Just trust,' Matt said. 'You've played your part. Now it's up to your family whether they'll have you back. You can't do any more.'

'Thank you.'

'It's cool.'

'And thanks for praying.'

'That's cool, too.'

A few carols later, and there was a moment of silence in the cab.

'You know,' Jake said, 'I have come to see in the last two years how important faith is to people.'

'Have you?'

'Yes, well, besides you… obviously … there was the guy in the casino called Father Jim. Then there was this Pentecostal pastor and his wife…'

'Go on.'

'And then there was Christine.'

Jake sighed.

'She was homeless, like me. She was deeply spiritual. She loved Christmas carols, just like you, and knew many of them by heart. She was one of the kindest people I have ever met. She became my friend.'

170

Jake paused.

'In the end,' he faltered, 'she… she gave her life… for me.'

'When?' Matt asked.

Jake turned to look at Matt, his eyes pleading, his heart breaking again.

'Tonight, Matt. She died for me. She chose to lay down her life for a no-good desperado like me.'

Jake saw the sadness in the trucker's eyes.

'She threw herself in the path of a car so that it wouldn't kill me, so that I could get to go home.'

For the next few minutes, the two men stared into the inky darkness and said nothing. There were no words, no carols, only the sound of the engine.

'I'm going to have to stop soon,' Matt said. 'There's a lorry park near here. It's got a trucker's cafe. We'll kip in here and then use the diner in the morning.'

'Okay,' Jake said.

Within ten minutes Matt had parked, turned off the ignition and the headlights, and turned the cab into what he had that evening called 'a home from home'.

Behind the seats in the cab there was a concealed bed where the driver slept. Matt was insistent that Jake had the bed, adding that he would quite happily sleep across the front seats and had done so many times before.

Jake was too tired to argue, so he climbed through and hid himself under a rich red duvet covered in laughing snowmen with ties made of holly.

Matt drew a thick black curtain from left to right across every window in the front of the cab and then took two mugs from a small cupboard above his head. He took a carton of fresh milk from a small fridge at Jake's feet and then added some hot chocolate. Jake watched as Matt reached up above the steering wheel and pulled open another compartment, revealing a small microwave oven.

'We've got all the mod cons,' Matt chortled.

Moments later, Matt had removed the two steaming mugs, adding sugar and marshmallows, before passing one to Jake.

'I'm really impressed,' Jake said. 'My only surprise is that you aren't serving Coca Cola.'

Matt chuckled.

'If you want some, we can always open up the back and see if they've left a bottle or two.'

'No thanks,' Jake laughed.

'Good night, my friend,' the trucker said. 'I'll turn the lights out in a moment. I'm just rigging up my DVD player to watch the end of a movie before I go to sleep. I'm going to finish one of my old favourites tonight. *It's a Wonderful Life*. I got halfway last night. I've been saving the best part for tonight. Sleep well.'

'Same to you,' Jake replied.

Jake looked up at the ceiling of the cab, where he could make out photographs of Matt with his wife and children. One caught his eye, of Matt in summertime, wearing a brown, sleeveless polo shirt, holding both his daughters.

I used to be a dad like that, he thought.

―――

Jake slept a full eight hours before he was woken up by the sound of Christmas carols playing once again. He rubbed his eyes as the low light of Christmas Eve morning was breaking through the windows of the cab, whose pitch-black curtains had now been drawn and tied back.

'Morning,' Matt exclaimed, as he popped his head above the driver's seat to look at Jake. 'The weather's slightly better. If we have breakfast and get you cleaned up, we can get underway while we have some light and get you home.'

'That sounds good to me,' Jake replied, brushing aside the duvet and climbing through to the front of the cab next to Matt.

'What do you want to do first?' Matt asked. 'Clean up or eat?'

'I'd like to clean up, if that's okay. It's been a long time since I've had a proper shower and I don't want to smell bad if I'm going to see my wife and kids tonight.'

'I'm kind of glad you said that,' Matt smiled.

'Hey,' Jake exclaimed, 'are you implying that I smell?'

'Everyone smells, Jake,' Matt replied. 'It's just that you smell – well, how shall I put it? If you don't do something about it, your family will very likely smell you before they see you, especially if they're downwind.'

Jake laughed.

Matt said, 'I'm going to take you through to the shower room at the back of the cafe. You just take your time. You can borrow my shower gel. It will make you smell like a prince. And breakfast is on me. My treat.'

'What about my beard?' Jake asked.

'I'm afraid I don't have anything that could possibly take care of that,' Matt chuckled. 'You'll just have to keep it for the time being.'

Matt switched off the carols and both men climbed down from the cab. They walked between the parked-up trucks and across the icy parking lot towards a one-storey building with warm lights and a sign with the words 'Night Owl Cafe' written above the entrance. Matt led Jake through the open dining area to the washrooms. The shower cubicle was unoccupied, so Jake removed his clothes and placed them on a chair. He closed the glass door and switched on the water.

Jake stood for several minutes relishing the long-lost joy of hot water on his head, flowing down across his beard, over his body to his feet. He took the shower gel from Matt's wash bag and began to clean his grimy body.

He washed and then dried his body on a fresh towel. He brushed his teeth and put on his clothes again. It felt strange being so clean inside such filthy clothes.

Jake walked back into the restaurant, found Matt sitting at a round small table beside a window looking out onto his Coca Cola Christmas truck, and returned the wash bag.

'Man,' Matt said. 'You smell good!'

'I feel good too,' Jake replied.

Matt picked up the breakfast menu. 'What do you fancy?'

'Whatever you're having, Matt.'

Matt called over to the waitress and ordered.

As Jake settled into his chair, he noticed a slim TV monitor on the wall. It was showing the morning news programme, with subtitles rather than sound. As he looked past Matt's huge shoulders, he saw the words BREAKING NEWS in red at the bottom of the screen. The headline read, TWO MEN ARRESTED IN CONNECTION WITH CASINO MURDER.

He watched as cameras panned in on an arrest taking place outside a large mansion with pillars. Police officers were trying to make their way out of the front door to the drive, but had met an incoming tide of reporters. Cameras were flashing as one by one the arresting officers emerged, eventually bringing two men out into the open.

Jake shuddered.

'Are you okay, brother?' Matt asked.

'It's them,' Jake said.

'Who?'

As Matt turned to look at the TV, the appearance of the two suspects became clearer. Before they were submerged in the sea of journalists, Jake saw and recognised them. There, with his unmistakable top hat and long black coat, was the Undertaker, in handcuffs, being led towards a police van, and just behind him, his boss.

'Bloody murderers,' Jake said.

That moment the cooked breakfast arrived: two fried eggs, sunny side up, three rashers of bacon, two halves of fried tomatoes, a large spoonful of well-cooked mushrooms, a pool of baked beans, enough toast to feed a family of five and the statutory trucker's beef burger lying in the place of honour on top of everything.

'I'm going to say one of my favourite graces,' uttered Matt.

Jake bowed his head.

'Okay, here it is. You ready?'

'Yep.'

'Lord, give us the grace and us the power to shift this lot in half an hour.'

Matt laughed and then dived into his food. Jake, however, was eating only tiny morsels.

'Come on, brother,' Matt said. 'Eat up.'

'I feel a bit sick after watching that news report.'

'Well, you need to build up your strength. You have a long day ahead.'

Jake lifted some bacon to his mouth.

'Not without maple syrup,' Matt said, taking a bottle from the table and squeezing it over Jake's rashers.

Jake ate a little, and then ate some more. He had never tasted bacon like it.

Within half an hour they had both finished everything and were leaning back on their chairs, patting their satisfied, swollen stomachs.

'I'll settle up and then we need to go,' Matt said. 'We'll do five hours and then have another break. Then I'll get you as near to your street as I can. It would be great if you could be home before Christmas Day.'

Jake nodded and the two men went to the counter, where Matt paid the bill. They left the diner, clambered back into the cab, and began their journey, further and further away from the northern lights.

———

For a long time, it was all Christmas carols and no conversation, except for some CB radio calls from other drivers who were eyeing up the Coca Cola Christmas truck and offering a mixture of admiration and banter. Jake, meanwhile, was deep in thought, contemplating the uncertain reunion which lay ahead. An hour or so of further silence and Jake's sense of apprehension was now palpable.

'You know,' Matt said, trying to distract Jake. 'I've carried some interesting cargo in my time. One time, I remember not knowing what was in the back of my truck. I picked up a large container sent from Australia. All it had on my artillery were the words 'Personal Belongings'. I knew the owner was waiting for me at the other end. When I arrived at my destination, he was like an excited boy.'

'What was it?' Jake asked.

'When I opened the truck, there inside was a purple and grey, two-toned 1961 Chevrolet Corvette. It was a fantastic looking car. He'd been desperate to be reunited with his pride and joy and was over the moon.'

'I suppose you've had some strange moments,' Jake mused.

'I have. A few years ago, I had to carry a cargo from a Scandinavian country at Christmas time. It contained about twenty full-size wooden reindeers, destined for an Earl's country estate. They were very realistic.'

'Did they have bells?' Jake asked laughing.

Matt laughed too before continuing. 'I picked them all up at about 2 a.m. During the journey, the back of the container came undone on the motorway and every single one of the statues fell out the back. What's worse, they all had weighted legs and landed upright on the lanes of the motorway behind my lorry. I had no idea that I'd lost them.'

'What happened?'

'Well, a few hours later I stopped for my compulsory break and a fellow trucker asked me, "Have you heard the news?" I answered, "What news?" He told me that one of the motorways from the docks had been blocked because a herd of reindeer had been found walking across the lanes at 3 a.m.'

'Oh no!'

'Oh yes! I went to the back of my truck, found it open, and all my cargo gone. I phoned up the office and reported that the reindeer were mine. The man on the other end of the phone said he needed to call the RSPCA. I said, "But they're statues!" The man, however, was insistent. He said that the person who'd phoned the office had told him they were walking!'

They were both laughing now.

'I asked him if he'd been drinking but he didn't reply. I'm forty-six, I've been driving for twenty years, and that's the strangest moment I've ever had!'

'That's funny,' Jake said.

'That's not the end of it either. Ever since, my nickname and CB call sign in the trucking community has been… well, you guess.'

'Rudolph?'

'Exactly.'

When the laughter subsided, Jake muttered, 'I think I probably qualify as strange cargo.'

'Don't worry,' Matt said. 'I've had all sorts travelling in this cab with me.'

With that, the sound of carols filled the air again.

Jake drifted in and out of sleep until they stopped for another break. Morning turned to afternoon and afternoon turned to early evening as the truck made its way towards Jake's destination.

And then, the moment came.

Matt said, 'We're nearly there, my friend.'

Jake looked at his watch. 10 p.m.

It was dark outside but he could see the signs indicating that the junction closest to his home was only about fifteen miles away.

'Listen, I can't take you all the way, but I will get you as close as I possibly can.'

'That's okay,' Jake answered. 'My house is only a mile away from the next junction. If you could drop me off there, you'll be able to join the motorway again.'

'That's cool with me,' Matt said.

Matt turned to look at Jake, his eyes filled with kindness. 'It's been good to meet you, Jake. I'll be praying for you as I drive the remainder of my journey.'

'I need all the prayer I can get. I don't think I've ever felt so weak and powerless in all my life.'

'Sometimes,' Matt said, 'we have to reach the end of our rope before miracles can happen.'

'It's going to be a miracle if my family are even there – and an even greater miracle if they welcome me back.'

'Well, miracles do happen. And I have seen stranger things than reindeer on the motorway.'

'That's reassuring,' Jake whispered.

'One more thing,' said Matt. 'If you're going to be seeing your wife and kids, you need to take them some presents. It's Christmas Eve, after all.'

'I don't have anything to give them.'

'I can do something about that.'

Matt looked into the rear-view mirror.

'If you look under the bed in the back, you'll find a drawer with presents.'

'Presents?'

'Every Christmas I take gifts to the local children's hospital where I live. So, here's what I want you to do. Take some presents. Take one for your wife – the mum's gifts have yellow ribbons on them. Take two for your boys. They're the ones with blue ribbons on them.'

Matt paused before adding, 'And take one of the presents with a pink ribbon.'

'Okay. Thank you, Matt.'

It took only a few moments for Jake to lift the mattress up behind him and retrieve an armful of presents.

'There are sacks in the back. Take one of those.'

Jake reached round behind him, took what looked like an old potato sack and popped his new gifts into it.

'Matt, I really owe you.'

'You owe me nothing, man. In fact, I'd like to give you a few more things. Take the warm blanket you were sleeping under last night. It's cold out there and you can't walk home in just a sweater and scarf. Wrap that around you.'

As Jake muttered his thanks, the signboard for his junction appeared out of the darkness on the side of the motorway.

Half a mile to go.

And then the gigantic, illuminated truck began to slow down as Matt applied the brakes, indicated that he was turning, manoeuvred up the slip road about half way up, and ground to a halt.

Jake draped the red blanket over his weary shoulders and took the sack of presents in one hand. He was about to leave the cab when Matt turned to him and said, 'Look Jake, every so often we lose our way, but it's coming home that really matters.'

Jake nodded.

Matt took his right hand off the steering wheel and stretched it out towards Jake. As he did, he caught part of his sleeve which rode up his arm, revealing a large tattoo. As Jake reached out his own hand, he saw the picture that Matt's cotton shirt had been concealing.

It was an angel with vast white wings looking plaintively down at a word written beneath. Jake felt his heart begin to surge and his eyes begin to fill. It was not the look of indescribable tenderness on the angel's face that broke him, but the single word in deep brown letters, in capitals, beneath the angel's feet.

MERCY.

Jake shook Matt's hand and swivelled round, opening the door of the cab, and climbing down after closing it.

He walked away from the truck and as he did, he waited for the sound of the great engine behind him to fire up again.

But he heard nothing.

After a few more metres he turned to wave, but as he looked down the sloping lane towards the motorway, there was no sign of the truck.

It had completely disappeared.

Matt had gone.

And for Jake, the moment of truth had come.

Hey Dad

I cant believe it!
Mummy told us you are coming home
Ive listened to the answer machine so many times
I cry every time I hear your voice
Though I don't let Bobby see me
Mummy is really nervous
Bobby is angry – but Sharma is really good with him
Theyve been going out a year now
This may be my last letter to you
Im only writing cos Im waiting for you
And Im all excited
Its very cold outside so Ive got your coat and shoes together
ready in case you need them
I wonder if youll look the same
Mummy says we mustn't expect you to be like you were
You may have changed
You may have got very poor and look bad
But I don't care
All I want is for you to come home
The best Christmas present in the world is you
I am going to the window now
Don't be long
We have a big surprise for you!
I love you

Tommy xxxxxxxxx

5. The End of It All

Trudging up the slip road with his sack of presents and his red blanket draped around him, Jake looked like a bedraggled Santa.

A few strides later and he came to a familiar landmark – an old brick railway bridge where he and his boys had often watched the trains passing underneath them. He squinted towards the fields adjacent and remembered the many hours he had spent with his boys searching for ancient artefacts in the mud. Their village had been built on what had originally been an ancient settlement, so was a promising quarry for amateur archaeologists. Their best find had been a flint axe and an arrowhead that had turned out to be 7,000 years old. On one occasion, Jake and his boys had bought a metal detector. The boys had been elated when their studious sweeping had uncovered a fistful of coins from the Iron Age. It seemed like yesterday.

The first house after the bridge was covered in hundreds of tiny Christmas lights, alternating blue and white, winking at Jake as he walked through the outskirts of the village. He marched across Station Road onto Church Lane. As he did so, a sudden gust of wind blew loose snow and ice from left to right across the road in front of him. Jake felt the freezing blast upon his face and sensed his energy begin to drain again. The exhaustion of anticipation was sapping him. Every muscle in his frail body now seemed to ache.

A bus shelter afforded momentary relief. Jake crouched there for several minutes, gathering the red blanket tightly around his skinny frame. Someone had written on the glass, 'Carl', then a love heart with an arrow through it, and the name 'Jodie'. Underneath one of them had penned the words, 'yours forever'.

Jake wondered if they were still together.

Realising that he needed to keep moving, he took off from his glassy sanctuary. All he could think of was home. A few moments later and he arrived at the Methodist Church, a one storey 1960s building with windows that had been covered on the inside by hand-painted paper scenes from the nativity story. Jake stopped and studied the pictures, which had evidently been painted by the church's children. The compositions had been cut to fit each window pane and were designed as imitation stained glass windows. They were drawn primarily in blue and yellow colours and showed cheerful scenes under crescent moons and luminescent stars.

As Jake prepared to move off towards the heart of the village, his eyes were drawn to a poster, encased in glass, on a wooden board by the side of the church. It contained a picture of a manger on it and some words. 'It's time for a stable relationship'.

Even from the edge of the village Jake could hear the parish church bells pealing, issuing an early summons to midnight communion. Jake walked towards the sound.

The houses on his route were decked with lights. Some were decorated with white lights hanging on strings. Others had multicoloured pine cone lights – gold and green, pink and blue, bright white and warm white. There were fairy lights and twinkle lights, curtain lights and net lights. Some of the houses had illuminated silhouettes of Christmas trees and Santas, snowflakes and snowmen. Others had bright white icicle displays, hanging from their roofs. One home had a large silhouette of a trumpeting angel fastened to its chimney stack and a white twinkling tree on the front lawn.

Several neighbours – keen not to be outshone by the other – had bought outdoor blossom trees whose branches glowed with LED lights. One family had decided to put their Christmas tree in the front yard. Snow hung on its branches, already made heavy by the neon minarets and beaded chains, teardrop lights and golden bells, gaudy baubles and grinning snowmen. And it boasted a tree topper to top all tree toppers – an iridescent starburst, glittered and sequinned, pulsating with a light that seemed whiter than the snow.

Jake moved from the treacherous pavement to the firmer, steadier surface of the asphalt on the road. There were no vehicles driving tonight. Snow-laden cars were lodged in their driveways both sides of the road, resting alongside wheelie bins that stood behind wooden gates with their numbers still visible.

Jake tramped past a traffic cone lying on its side and came to the village post office. The old letterbox with its royal crest was still rooted where it had been for decades. A red post office van was parked out the front, where he noticed a poster advertising a local dry-cleaning business. He frowned as he saw that the village store next door had been turned into a hair and beauty salon.

As he advanced, he caught sight of the only pub in the village - the King's Arms. A golden glimmer was coming from the building, glowing as it was with a darker lamp than the bright white lights shining from the houses leading to it. Jake increased his pace, drawn by the golden, shimmering lights.

On his way, he happened upon a solitary walker with a Blenheim coloured King Charles Spaniel. The dog had left its lead and was prancing with playful exuberance, biting at the snow before shaking his head and tossing it out of his mouth. The dog saw Jake and leaped up at him, the paws of both front legs resting for a moment upon his knees. His glistening eyes seemed to be almost bursting with vitality. For a moment, Jake remembered the German Shepherd that had kept him safe and warm in the north, and grief filled his soul.

Jake noticed a bright white Porsche, brand new, with a snowy mullet, parked in the gravel driveway of a house with Roman columns at its entrance. The car had a personalised number plate.

He passed two tall, semi-detached, thatched cottages, originally built for the tenants of the local earl's estate. These houses were older than most of the others in the village. Most of the houses had been built in the 1960s. These dated from the nineteenth century and had cast iron Victorian lampposts illuminating their wooden gates.

For many years before he ran away, Jake used to covet these cottages, hoping one day to have enough money to buy and occupy one of them with his family. That dream seemed hollow now.

A few moments later and he struggled to the car park of the King's Arms, whose sign was flapping noisily in the wind. A blackboard stood outside the front, advertising live music and a new menu, and promoting Christmas bookings and a New Year's Eve supper and dance. Jake noticed that the faded green wooden shutters hadn't been replaced. He had always liked them; they reminded him of a French farmhouse he once visited where he had enjoyed the best meal of his life – escargots, salad, fish, steak, a gourmet selection of desserts, a glorious array of cheeses, liqueurs and the finest rich ground coffee he had ever tasted.

Jake lifted the cold and uncooperative latch and opened the door into the pub.

He was in a small hallway with another door a few metres in front of him, leading into the main bar. On his right, there was a window onto an alcove, containing a large round table where young men were drinking beer and playing cards. One of them was dressed in a white jumper with a red reindeer on it. They were wearing woollen Santa hats.

Jake stamped his shoes on the mat, forcing the snow and icicles from his feet, clapping his hands and loosening the snowflakes from his tattered mittens.

For several minutes, he stayed there all alone, enjoying the heat in the passageway. But then the inside door opened.

Someone with an unlit Cuban cigar in a bejewelled hand was on his way to join a group of people smoking in an outdoor enclosure.

Jake froze.

It was Pete Marley.

Pete tried to get past.

For a moment, Jake looked at Pete. And then it struck him. Pete did not recognise him. How could he? Jake's hair was long and dirty. He had a bristling, heavy beard and was covered from his shoulders to his knees in a bright red blanket. He was camouflaged by months of destitution.

Jake was about to speak when Pete put his hand into his pocket and drew out a pound coin.

'Here,' he said, adding, 'good luck to you, Santa,' before navigating his way to the door, letting the cold night air into the lobby.

Jake stood gawping at the coin now settled in the centre of his palm. Disgusted, he strode out of the pub, turning away from the smoking fraternity, hurling the coin with disdain into a drain. All the while the sound of the church bells grew louder.

As Jake turned the corner he saw the most pathetic of trees, its fragile form made visible by a street lamp right beside it. It had scrawny, twisted branches that looked like gangling arms, and tangled knots of spindly twigs like mats of unkempt hair. The wind tore through its snow-flecked boughs, whining and wailing.

A few steps on and he had left the village hall behind and arrived at the sports club. Its lights were on and Jake could see giddy people conversing, raising their glasses to each other as a DJ played familiar, Christmas hits.

A few metres later and Jake saw on the left side of the road a quaint old cottage. It was like something out of a nursery tale. It had a three foot, glass illuminated reindeer standing in front of the wooden front door. The entire porch was lit up by a hundred fairy lights, revealing a brass knocker in the shape of a roaring lion and a holly wreath hanging underneath. Ivy was creeping up the wall around four latticed windows, reaching up towards octagonal chimney pots, venting smoke from an open fire inside.

Jake wondered if 'Granny Freda', as his family called her, still lived there. She used to be a babysitter for his boys. She had been a student at Oxford and had graduated with honours, pursuing a career in academic life. One night he and Sally had returned from dinner in the pub to find her sitting on their sofa reading to Billy from a book entitled, 'Teach Yourself Serbo Croat', and reciting Slavic sounding words to him. Jake strained his eyes to see if she was in, but even though the lights were on his view was hindered by the blinds.

Jake strode on towards a line of pine trees which he knew stood watch over the graves in the cemetery of the village church.

St Joseph's was arguably the pride and joy of the village, even among those who never went to services there. It had an ancient, embattled tower whose base dated to the twelfth century. The clock was set there in the early 1600s and was renowned for keeping very accurate time, though oddly it had stopped for once, at six o'clock.

Jake passed through the lichgate. In former times, corpses would be carried to the gate and placed there upon a bier. The priest used the gate to shelter from the rain – although in the year of the Black Death the priest might himself have been the corpse. When the plague hit the village, it killed four vicars in under a year.

Jake proceeded under the pitched, triangular roof of the wooden gate and made his way into the graveyard, the gravel crunching under his feet.

Everywhere he looked there were mossy crosses, slabs and headstones, some of them accompanied by dilapidated angels with eyes fixed in a dreamy, upward gaze towards the heavens.

A statue of a curly-haired cherub with a fat face stood in the right corner of the graveyard underneath a yew tree, a finger at his lips as if enjoining everyone to reverent silence. The boy, who had been carved with a slightly impish look, was the proud owner of a pair of undersized wings and an oversized belly.

Jake wondered for a moment, had the cherub been real, if he would ever have made it off the ground.

He stepped under the shade of the yew tree and past the portly cherub to a gravestone he had often visited in secret in times gone by. Sally's father was buried there. Her family were locals, born and bred. They were not 'comers' like Jake, a word a few of the more parochial locals sometimes used to describe newcomers to their village. Sally's dad had not been like that with Jake. He had taken him to his heart and treated him like the son he had never had. Jake had loved him, often slipping out to have a pint of golden ale with him at the King's Arms, asking him for the wisdom gained from years as a railwayman and, during the war, as a soldier in the Far East.

Jake looked at the headstone, with its brief and mournful eulogy to a loving husband and a doting dad and grandfather. As he did, he thought of the legacy of his lamentable life and fell to his knees in the snow.

'Stan,' Jake stuttered. 'I'm really sorry... I let you down... I let Sally down... she deserved better... you deserved better... I hope, if you're listening, you can forgive me... I want to make you proud of me again... If you can hear me, please give me strength... strength to go home... strength to put things right.'

Jake took one last look at the gravestone. As he gazed down at the long slab beneath him, he noticed a fresh holly wreath.

Jake's heart broke.

'I miss you Dad. I miss you so much it hurts.'

As the tears fell once again from his face into the snow, a gust of wind blew through the flat, green leaves in the branches of the yew tree above his head. And for a moment he swore he heard a whisper in the boughs, uttered between the pealing of the bells. 'I'll be your father now.'

Jake had no idea how long he had knelt and cried in the chiaroscuro of the yew tree grotto. What brought him round was the increasing noise of trudging steps upon the gravel path leading to the entrance of the church, accompanied by the sound of intermittent laughter. When the church bells stopped, Jake heard singing breaking through the fissures of the porch and stained glass windows, carried on by the wind to where he knelt, as if calling out to him.

He got up, wiping the snow from his wet knees, before taking the hessian sack of presents and his red blanket and hiding them behind a tall standing gravestone.

He walked towards the oak front door of the church, grasped the oval iron handle, and turned it. The door opened, its creaking covered by the sound of many voices singing.

Once inside, he saw guttering candles blazing everywhere, in every window and on every shelf on both sides of the building.

Jake found a tiny plastic chair – intended for a child in Sunday school – and sat on it right at the back of the church, a few metres away from the nearest pew of Christmas worshippers.

The carol ended and a warden in a tailored suit started to read the lesson.

In the beginning was the Word, and the Word was with God, and the Word was God. All things were made by him; and without him was not anything made that was made.

Jake looked beyond the reader to the rood screen separating the sanctuary from the nave. It had a medieval painting depicting Joseph at the birth of the Christ child.

In him was life; and the life was the light of men. And the light shineth in darkness; and the darkness comprehended it not. He was in the world, and the world was made by him, and the world knew him not. He came unto his own, and his own received him not. And the Word was made flesh, and dwelt among us, (and we beheld his glory, the glory as of the only begotten of the Father,) full of grace and truth.

Even the revellers from the King's Arms fell silent as the words echoed through the building.

Jake looked beyond the screen at the choir stalls, where twelve men and women and four young people in their early teens sat with solemn faces in their red robes and white surpluses. The chancel steps were covered in a golden carpet leading right up to the high altar, which was draped in a gold and white embroidered altar cloth. Three silver chalices and patens were lying on it, a silver cross standing in front of them all.

Jake spotted an illuminated nativity scene just to the right of the rood screen.

Joseph was in front of the manger, looking with devotion at the baby there.

No man hath seen God at any time, the only begotten Son, which is in the bosom of the Father, he hath declared him.

A moth hovered around a light bulb above Jake's head as the reader released his tight hold of the eagles' wings of the lectern and walked with to the end of a pew where he sat down.

The congregation stood and sang another carol.

As the carol ended, Jake watched as the vicar in his black cassock, white surplus and golden preaching scarf ascended the steps of the ancient pulpit and stood with reverence, bowing his head. He was in his late sixties, Jake surmised, and had a full head of grey hair and a plump face with rosy cheeks. He prayed a formal prayer, asking that his words would be acceptable in God's sight, and then the congregation sat as the vicar preached.

Right at the beginning of his address, he drew out a brand-new pack of playing cards. They had been a gift from his young grandchildren, who he had taught to play cards. On the back of each card was a picture of a fat, dancing Santa.

'Imagine,' he said, 'receiving a gift like this and finding one card missing, say, the King of Hearts. There would still be fifty-one out of the fifty-two cards but this one absent card would always leave you frustrated, because this one card makes all the difference.'

The vicar went on to talk about life being like a deck of cards. We all get dealt different hands and we all deep down want to play the game of life and play it well. 'But if the King of Hearts is missing, there will always be a gap, a void, a hole,' he said.

Then the vicar talked about Christmas, about the birth of Jesus as the birth of the King of kings, and Jesus himself as the kindest and most compassionate man who has ever graced the stage of history. The King of Hearts, no less.

'Whatever you do,' he concluded, 'make sure you give a special place in your life to him. He makes all the difference.'

As the vicar stepped down, the choristers stood up. The organist had moved from the sanctuary to the north wall of the church, where he sat at a Clavinova piano flanked by three musicians – one with a violin, one with a flute and one with an oboe. After a pause, he began to play a familiar melody. The singers soon joined in with the musicians.

O holy night! The stars are brightly shining,
It is the night of the dear Saviour's birth.

Many began to hum along, especially as the choristers sang,

Fall on your knees! Oh hear the angel voices!

As the carol proceeded to its final verse, some of the people in front of Jake began to stand up and sing with gusto.

Christ is the Lord! Then ever, ever praise we,
His power and glory evermore proclaim!
His power and glory evermore proclaim!

By the time the last line came, nearly everyone was standing. Except Jake, that is. His head was bowed low, almost to his knees. His body felt enfolded by invisible arms.

As the candles flickered in the breezy church, a voice began to emerge from somewhere deep within him. No one heard it except Jake, and the one to whom he spoke.

'I surrender,' he said.

The vicar now presided at the holy table, working his way through the words of the Eucharistic liturgy, until he raised a chalice in both hands and said, 'Tonight, many people drink to forget. We drink to remember.'

Over the next five minutes, most of the people in the church began to make their way to the altar to kneel on faded hassocks at the wooden rail, receiving bread and wine.

Jake waited until the people in the row in front of him processed towards the chancel steps and used the opportunity to make a quiet exit. He stood for a moment outside, staring at the stars as he shoved the woollen hat on his head. He took the red blanket and the sack of presents from their hiding place and flung them over his shoulder.

It was time to go home.

He left through the lichgate and worked his way down the road to the turning onto the estate where he used to live. He made his way along the crescent, past two-storey houses on his left and bungalows on his right.

In the final bend before his house, he noticed that there were white sparkling lights in almost every window. One house bucked the trend by hanging bright blue lights. It had a spacious lobby with expansive windows. An illuminated snowman was smiling at him through the windowpane. A bright red scarf was draped around his neck. He had red mufflers over his ears, a broom in his hand, round black buttons down his front, and a black top hat with a green band around it. A banner with the words HOME, SWEET HOME was hanging just above his head.

Jake smiled.

As he turned the corner, he could now see his former home about two hundred metres on the left side of the street.

His heart was thumping hard. He thought of running but he had been a fugitive for a long time now. He began the final steps.

Just then, a front door opened on his right and an elderly couple came out and stood together arm-in-arm at the porch of their bungalow, waving to him. He recognised them straightaway. Fred and Ethel had been good neighbours, always asking Jake how his children were doing at school.

'Go Jake, go,' Fred said.

Jake trembled.

A door on his left opened and a man with a fur trimmed Santa hat with the words BAH HUMBUG on it walked out onto his path and shouted, 'Welcome home, mate.' Again, Jake recognised him. It was Jim, a man with whom he had propped up the bar of the King's Arms many times.

Jim was followed by three men with beer cans in their hands who sang a football chant, altering the words, shouting, 'Jakey's coming home!'

A window opened and two pre-teen girls with reindeer headbands pulled some party poppers which exploded in a loud crack, firing tiny multicoloured streamers into the air like paper fireworks. Even though they had grown taller and more confident, Jake knew they were friends of Tommy's.

Another of Tommy's friends appeared from the front door of his home, blowing a silver foil trumpet. He was with his father, wearing a glittering silver top hat and urging Jake on.

Jake was seconds away from his front door.

Just then, Jake looked up. In an upstairs window of his house, now thirty metres away, he could just discern the outline of a boy looking out from behind a festive, seven branch light display.

As soon as Jake saw him, the curtain twitched and closed.

Within a few seconds, or so it seemed, the front door of Jake's house swung open and there was Tommy. He looked older than his eight years – his hair was longer, he was taller, and his body leaner than before. He was wearing some of Bobby's clothes – a patterned sweater, navy polo shirt and a pair of worn-out black school shoes.

Tommy ran, his arms outstretched.

Jake dropped his sack.

He watched as his son raced towards him, his arms reaching out.

They were holding something.

Tommy paused before his dad as more neighbours came out onto the street.

'Is that you, Dad?'

Jake pulled off his hat and took off his makeshift cloak.

Tommy smiled.

'Here Dad,' he said, 'I thought you might need these.'

Tommy's hands presented a pair of shoes, Jake's favourite shoes before he ran away from home – a pair of luxury, chestnut coloured loafers in textured vintage calf leather.

Jake kicked off his trainers and slipped the shoes onto his feet.

'Here,' said Tommy, 'don't forget this.'

Tommy pushed something else towards his father – something dark on which the loafers had been resting. As soon as Jake touched it, he knew what it was. It was his black cashmere greatcoat.

He took it in his hands and put it on. He had lost so much weight living rough that the coat hung loose, even over a thick woollen sweater and several layers of shirts.

Wrapping himself within its soft fabric, Jake took his son in his arms and hugged him.

He was speechless.

And he was weeping.

Jake had not wanted to let Tommy go – not for a long time – but his front door had now opened again.

It was Billy's turn now.

But Billy wasn't carrying anything. And Billy didn't look excited or relieved. He looked angry. He was a good foot taller than when Jake last had seen him, and wider too. He had obviously started working out and his biceps were visible even underneath his jacket.

'I don't know how you can do that, Tommy?' Billy shouted. 'Not after all he's done to us.'

Billy made a move towards his father, raising his fist to strike him.

Jake knew his older son would have hit him hard and true had Tommy not been there, turning to his brother, raising his arm to protect his dad.

'No, Billy!' another, older voice joined in.

Jake knew instantly who it was.

Sally.

She had now come out of the house and was standing right behind Billy, holding back his arm, speaking firmly to him.

'That is not the answer.'

Billy lowered his arm and looked at his mother, before skulking off towards a neighbour's house, where he fell into the arms of a teenage girl.

'Sorry about that,' Sally said. 'It's all too raw for him.'

'That's okay,' Jake stuttered. 'I deserve it.'

Sally was now standing in front of Jake in a long, familiar beige raincoat. It was now showing signs of wear and tear, but she wasn't. She did not look a day older. She looked beautiful.

Sally stood with her hands in her coat pockets, looking at him. 'I have a Christmas present for you,' she said softly, withdrawing a tiny object from her pocket.

Jake looked and saw it gleaming in the half light of the street.

It was a ring – the same as the one that he had thrown at her in the kitchen two years before.

'Why the hell are you giving him that?' Billy shouted from the shadows.

'Because love is a choice,' Sally said. 'And I choose love.'

As Jake heard those words, he fell to his knees in the snow and leaned forward into Sally's waist, his arms around her fast, weeping.

Sally reached down and held him by the shoulders, nestling her nose into his tangled hair.

'It's okay, darling,' she said.

After several minutes, Jake released his hold and tilted back. He had been aware of something or someone pawing his hands at his wife's back.

Just as he wondered who or what it was, a small, fair-haired girl emerged from behind, almost as if she had been hiding in her overcoat. She was wearing pink wellington boots and a shin-length navy mackintosh. She had a white woollen hat with a bobble on the top and two pigtails, tied by yellow ribbons.

'She's your daughter,' Sally said. 'Her name is Daisy.'

Jake started to cry again, leaving Daisy confused and on the edge of bursting into tears herself. Jake, seeing she was nervous, calmed himself. 'Daisy, I am your dad,' he said.

Jake remembered the extra gift that Matt had given him just an hour before and smiled. He uttered a quiet 'thank you' under his breath and then reached inside his sack and found the present wrapped in a pink ribbon.

'Here, this is for you, Daisy.'

Daisy took the present and dashed indoors, skipping as she went.

'And these are for you boys,' Jake said, handing several gifts to Tommy, instructing him to give one to his brother.

'And this is for you,' Jake said, lifting a present to his wife.

'Thank you, darling,' she said. 'And this, Jake, is for you...'

With that, Sally signalled to a scattered group of friends, neighbours and family members who were watching the drama of Jake's homecoming. Two of them took hold of a large white bedsheet, with WELCOME HOME painted in jerky red capitals, and hung it across the street using a stepladder and some string. They tied one end to a larch tree and the other to a weeping willow opposite.

The men with beer cans in their hands arrived with an oil drum cut in half, set them on a bed of bricks, then filled them with kindling, paraffin and crumpled newspaper. They set fire to the contents and added coal when the wood burst into flames. They then draped metal meshing across the top and, when the coal turned grey, started placing marinated turkey pieces and special, flavoured sausages on the improvised grills.

As the meat startled to sizzle above the glowing coal, the aroma of barbecued food began to fill the night air. Sally and three of her friends brought vegetables on trays – roasted parsnips, carrots and potatoes. One of their husbands carried a huge metal jug full of gravy made from turkey juices, chicken stock and cider. Another brought out some roasting trays on which to place the turkey and the sausages. The last of the men carried a stack of paper plates and plastic cups, accompanied by one of his children, who was carrying a bundle of Christmas crackers.

As Jake stood up, he wandered round the neighbourhood, bemused by his wife's forgiveness and his neighbours' kindness.

And he watched as Tommy ran from one person to another, telling them, 'I lost my Dad but look, I've found him again!'

A little later, sitting on a wall with a paper plate full of Christmas dinner, Jake felt exhausted. Sally left the trestle table where she was serving food and came to sit beside him. She carried a mug of steaming mulled wine with her.

'This will help,' she said.

'Thanks,' he said, sipping it, sensing an instant glow within.

'You know, Sally,' he added, 'I've been involved in terrible things. I'm not sure you'll feel the same once you know.'

'Look, Jake,' she answered, 'I've not entirely been innocent either.' She frowned for a moment, then smiled at him as she continued. 'But when I gave you that eternity ring just now, that was my way of saying that I'd rather focus on the future than the past.'

'You astound me,' Jake said.

'I astound myself,' Sally said, squeezing him as she did and laughing.

Through his tears, Jake looked with wonderment at the people milling around him in the snow, wielding plates and cups.

As he stared at them, he rubbed his eyes, as he swore he saw some familiar faces among his old friends and neighbours.

A man with jet black hair, raising a glass of whiskey as he laughed with a huge black man with tattooed skin.

And a young woman in a long great coat, her face turned away from them, talking in an animated way with no one in particular.

All the while, the thickening snow fell from the heavens, falling about the revellers, like bright white feathers.

About the Author

Mark Stibbe is the award-winning author of over 50 non-fiction books, many of them bestsellers and translated into foreign languages. Recently he has started writing fiction, most notably the first in the Thomas Pryce spy stories, *The Fate of Kings*. He is a full-time writer who also contributes to newspapers, magazines, TV and Radio.

Mark and his wife Cherith run *BookLab*, a business dedicated to helping good writers become great authors. He is in demand as a speaker and regularly leads writing workshops, with a strong emphasis on the importance and dynamics of storytelling. Mark currently lives with Cherith and their Black Labrador Bella in Kent.